CHEATERS

NINE STORIES THAT EXPLORE THE OTHER SIDE OF LOVE

NOVONEEL CHAKRABORTY

Penguin
metro reads

An imprint of Penguin Random House

PENGUIN METRO READS

USA | Canada | UK | Ireland | Australia
New Zealand | India | South Africa | China

Penguin Metro Reads is part of the Penguin Random House group of companies
whose addresses can be found at global.penguinrandomhouse.com

Published by Penguin Random House India Pvt. Ltd
7th Floor, Infinity Tower C, DLF Cyber City,
Gurgaon 122 002, Haryana, India

Penguin
Random House
India

First published in Penguin Metro Reads by Penguin Random House India 2018

Copyright © Novoneel Chakraborty 2018

All rights reserved

10 9 8 7 6 5 4 3 2 1

ISBN 9780143441977

Typeset in Adobe Garamond Pro by Manipal Digital Systems, Manipal
Printed at Thomson Press India Ltd, New Delhi

www.penguin.co.in

For each and every reader of mine, who has loved and appreciated my thrillers for a decade. Trust me, this short story collection was made possible only because of your continuous love and faith in me and my stories. Thank you!

Contents

Tickets Are Done

Night One

I'm at Dharamkot, near Mcleod Ganj, Himachal Pradesh. Everyone is in their rooms. By everyone else I mean the director, the director of photography, the producer, and me, the art director. We are here for a week-long film recce. Even though I'm in my room, I'm not able to fall sleep. In spite of being under two blankets, my legs drawn up to my chest, and wearing woollens, I can still feel the chill in my bones. We got this house through Airbnb; we have four rooms. But we only have basic amenities. Personally, I hate nights like these when sleep is a far cry and thoughts from the past hover over my mind. I did WhatsApp my husband, Raghav, but he is asleep. It's 2.30 a.m. What else will he do after working his ass off as a creative director in a premiere advertising agency in Mumbai. He has some important meeting early tomorrow morning. During nights like these I have a bad habit of revisiting my past. What happened, what couldn't happen and what could have happened. I've always been a reader. Especially of love stories. They made me believe, from a young age, that a person can only have one soulmate. But as I grew up, I realized there could be more than one. I've had two. The first destroyed me and the second created me.

His name is Kshay—the one who destroyed me. I've known many souls but none like Kshay. When he was with me, I could read it in his eyes that he couldn't be anywhere else. But the moment we parted ways, I knew he wouldn't try to get in touch with me ever. I had always been the one initiating things. It irked me. It pulled down my self-esteem. But I still did it. I did it for five long years. Then I told him I was done with him. But on nights like these I realize it's a lie. I'm not done with him. Maybe I'm done with his presence. But what about his absence? When you become way too wary of someone's absence, that too, is a kind of presence, isn't it? The realization was scary. It occurred to me when I was with Raghav one day. And I still felt lonely. The worst kind of loneliness is when you are with your lover and his warmth doesn't reach your heart. It made me aware of all the lies I had been telling myself. All the pretence I chose in order to 'move on'.

I still remember the day I met Kshay. It was so casual that I never could imagine that something special was in store for us. We were in a cafe. I was supposed to meet a friend. I had been waiting for her for some time and had gone to the washroom. And what do I see when I come out? The cappuccino that I had left on my table was being finished by a man. He was standing with his back to me. I found it weird. I went to him and told him it was my coffee. He was immediately apologetic. He thought it was his since he too had been to the washroom. He offered to buy me another coffee. I told him to chill and behaved as if it wasn't an issue. However, he was persistent. By then, my friend had arrived. I went with her to another cafe. That night around twelve, someone rang the doorbell. I opened the door and found a steaming cup of coffee on the floor and a post-it note on it that said: *Sorry, I followed you. But I had to get rid of the guilt. Here's your coffee. I swear I won't follow you again. But you can if you want to.*

There was a smiley and a phone number. I couldn't help but smile. A stranger following me the whole evening only to say sorry? It seemed so irresistibly romantic albeit a bit alarming. I took the note and the coffee. His face flashed in front of me. From just a stranger, he had suddenly turned into someone desirable. Honestly, I wanted to ping him right away but chose to wait. Two days later, I texted him with a smiley in the end:

Hey, if your guilt trip is over then you can text me. It's the coffee girl :)

There was no response. I felt as if I had expected a little too much. Almost a month later, when I had forgotten about him, I got a message:

The guilt trip's final destination is the coffee girl. Where do I find her? Any clue?

I didn't know what to say then. That's Kshay. You just can't bracket him into any kind of expectation.

I turn over, shivering. My eyes fall on the mirror across the bed. I'm smiling. His thoughts still make me smile. My smile tells me so much about my present self even though I haven't seen him for four years now. I dare not read too much into that smile. I close my eyes wondering how he looks now. Then a thought strikes me: what if he comes knocking at my door? And a few minutes later, I hear someone actually knocking at my door. I feel a thud in my heart. Maybe I'm imagining it. But I hear the knock again. I frown and get out of bed. My heart is beating fast. I open the door. It's a bearded man with shoulder-length hair; he's wearing black carbon framed specs. And has hypnotic eyes. It's Kshay!

* * *

Night Two

I stare at him. And he at me. Is this real or a figment of my imagination?

'I had a feeling that someone was stalking me. Didn't know it was you!' Kshay says.

'Oh, come on!' I say, finally realizing that what was happening was real.

'How did you know I'm here?' I ask.

'I didn't. I needed a cigarette. The owner said he didn't have any but one of you might. So . . .'

Of course, how stupid of me to ask. How would he *know* that I was here, I think, and say, 'I don't have cigarettes.'

'I know. You never smoked.'

The fact that he is so conclusive irritates me. What he said was true but still, one shouldn't be so certain about someone else.

'No. I do. But right now I don't have any.' I lie so he knows there's more to me than what he knows.

'Ah!' He raises his eyebrows.

'My colleagues may have some,' I say and step out of the room. It's freezing in the corridor. Kshay stays where he is. I go to the director's room and knock. When he opens the door, I ask for a cigarette. He is more than happy to give me a few. He offers company but I say I'm all right. I turn to find Kshay peeping inside my room. *Is he checking who I'm with?* I wonder.

'What happened?' I demand.

'Nothing,' he says and takes the cigarette from me. He has a lighter.

'You want to know if I'm alone here.' I try to sound smart. He lights his cigarette, looking curiously at me. I hate this look of his. It makes me uneasy. It did so before as well.

'Thanks,' he says and walks away. I want to call him. I don't. That's Kshay. He will approach you when you are least ready and leave you when you are totally ready.

I've a fitful sleep. The next day I leave with my team to find some good spots to shoot. We zero in on a house in Rakkar village. It's stunning, to say the least. In between, Raghav and I have a few phone calls but the network is patchy so we can't talk for a long time. I want to tell him that I met Kshay but I don't. He knows Kshay is my ex. When I had told Raghav about Kshay, I had edited a lot of that story. Whenever one is narrating something from one's past, the story never comes out the way it actually happened, no matter how hard one tries to be faithful to the facts. There's always something different that we end up introducing; or we omit something. I didn't mention last night's meeting because I didn't think it was important enough for Raghav to know. Had I mentioned it, he might have assumed that it had meant something to me. When it comes to confessing stuff to one's partner, one must second guess his or her reaction intelligently before spilling the beans.

We have lunch at a Tibetan restaurant in Mcleod Ganj; we check out the monastery close to the restaurant and in the evening, return to our house. The producer and the director go for trekking, while the director of photography prefers to stay back in his room. I was hoping to bump into Kshay during dinner but he wasn't there. I return to my room, have a hot water bath, dive under my blankets and call Raghav. Then I start watching a movie on my phone. Somewhere in between I stop, not able to focus. Truth be told, I was really hoping to bump into Kshay. I had thought I would find him downstairs during breakfast or in the town when we went for the recce. I felt that he was nearby but didn't see him. I hear footsteps outside my room. I wonder if it's Kshay. He is supposedly in a room nearby. I feel an urge to open my door and check. If it's him, I can always say that I wanted to take a stroll. I keep toying with the idea of leaving my bed when I hear a knock at my door. Exactly the way it had happened the previous night. It's enough to help me make a decision. I get out of bed and open the door. It's Kshay.

'Is it cigarettes again?' I ask sarcastically.

'I have a cigarette,' he says.

'Then what do you want?'

'You,' he smirks.

'What you need me for?' I ask. It's not that I don't want to go out. I just don't want to relent too easily.

'Care to join me for a smoke?' he asks. Another smirk. I try to look away before I lose myself a bit more.

* * *

Night Three

I follow Kshay outside. I know I have left my phone in the room but then who will call me at this time? We leave the house and walk till we reach a small open space. We stand against the iron railings; one can see the hilly road below and the snow-capped mountains in the distance. It's misty and the visibility is poor. Kshay sits down and lights his cigarette. He offers one to me. *Should I tell him I lied?* I wonder but take the cigarette. He helps me light it and then lights his. He takes a puff. I too take one. This isn't the first time I'm smoking so at least I don't make an utter fool of myself and cough when I inhale the smoke.

'So, what are you doing here?' I ask. The silence between us is becoming awkward with every passing second. He puffs out a cloud of smoke and says, 'Want to play a game?'

'A game?'

'Let's guess what we have been up to in the last four years.'

'Interesting. But what will we gain out of it?'

'What will we gain if we don't play it either?'

I stare at him. Does he remember why we broke off? It was because he was never direct about anything. Men like Kshay should never commit to any girl. Commitment is a destination and the moment men like him see it clearly, looming in the horizon, they change their tracks. He is like the wind. You can feel him, but you can't trap him and make him yours entirely. Only the bit which hits you stays with you. And you, in your innocence, assume that's the whole of him. No! He is an emotional tourist. Women should be careful of such men. But they always end up falling for them. Such men are conquests. Hopeless conquests to make nests with people who are inherently emotional vagabonds. I tried making that conquest for five years. And trust me, if there wasn't a society, any parental pressure on me to settle down, I would have continued. There's that heady feeling in pursuing someone. That's also because men like Kshay never tell you directly that they aren't with you for the long run. They keep you hanging. In that, I had developed a certain pleasure. Or so I had thought. Until, of course, Raghav happened.

'All right. Let's begin,' I say.

'Okay. The one major change is that you are married now,' he says. There is nothing in his voice or face to help me understand if this fact at all matters to him.

'That's easy, Kshay,' I say and add, 'At thirty-two, almost every other person in India is married.'

He smirks and says, 'Your turn.'

Kshay had never stuck to one job for a long time. Last time I knew, he was working with Discovery Channel as a line producer on a north-east India project. Before that he was the brand manager of a celebrity cricketer. And before that he was an investigative journalist. How he does all this

I have no idea. He once told me why he does it though. *One life—many desires.* That's his punchline of sorts.

'You have a different job now. And, of course, you aren't married.'

He looks at me for some time and then bursts out laughing.

'What?'

'That was so obvious,' he says.

'Just like your guess.'

'Okay, so should I guess something which is obvious to me but not to you?'

'Go on.'

Kshay comes a little closer. 'Your husband doesn't know you met me last night though he knows who I am.'

I swallow nervously, hoping he will not notice.

'He knows!' It's a reflex lie.

'He does?' Kshay looks at me intently.

'Whether he does or not is actually none of your business, Kshay. Not any more.'

'So he doesn't. The question is why not?'

'It's not important. We aren't doing anything.'

'Or is it because if he may think we are?'

'Please, Raghav isn't the possessive or the jealous type.'

'Give a man the right information and it won't take too long for him to start behaving in an entirely wrong manner.' His smirk is back. And I hate it. I don't know why exactly I do it, but I drop the cigarette. I stamp on it angrily and go back to my room. I pick my phone up, dial Raghav and while waiting for him to pick up, rush back to where Kshay is sitting.

'Hi, baby, sorry to disturb you. I forgot to tell you something. Last night I happened to meet Kshay. Remember, my ex? Yeah, he is here for some . . . I don't know what,' I say the last bit looking at Kshay. A deliberate look. I want him to know he isn't important. Not any more. I hear a sleepy Raghav ask me if there's anything else, otherwise he will talk to me tomorrow.

'He knows,' I say with a smile.

'Well, good to know that.'

I notice he has finished his cigarette.

'Can I be honest?' he asks.

'About?'

'You know why I wanted you to tell your husband about me?'

I frown.

'I didn't want to feel guilty.'

The frown deepens.

'Guilty about?'

Kshay smirks and walks away, whistling an old Hindi song. Like he always used to when he had something wicked on his mind. And he knows I always had a thing for his wickedness.

* * *

11

Night Four

I am with my team, checking out a few houses. We left after breakfast. Yet again I thought I would see Kshay but didn't. I called Raghav right after I woke up but he didn't pick up. I left a message but there has been no call. It's only when my team decides to have some steaming hot momos from a restaurant, recommended to us by a friend from Mumbai, that my phone flashes Raghav's name. I pick up. He sounds a little different. The way men do when they have something on their minds.

'You had breakfast?' he asks.

'I did. And now we are going to have some lip-smacking momos,' I say cheerfully.

'With Kshay?' he asks. It's so blunt and quick, almost as if he had that name on his mind for quite some time.

'Of course not. I'm with my team! Why would you say that?'

'If you can meet him in the middle of the night then in the daytime it is nothing, right?'

Raghav has never been curt with me. Not until this morning. Did the phone call change something? One bit of true information and a barrage of false assumptions? *Is our relationship that fragile?* I wonder and tell him that I'm indeed with my team. He pushes me for a video call. I take it as an offence.

'Why should I video call you? Why can't you trust me?'

'If you are not with him then why can't you video call? It's just a video call.'

No, it's not *just* a video call. It's a question of trust. The foundation of all relationships. I realize the call has ended. Before I can guess if it is a network issue or a deliberate action, I notice my phone is flashing Raghav's name again, but this time it's a video call. I feel extremely angry. I told him I'm not with Kshay; I said there's no point of a video call and yet he is calling me? Doesn't my word mean anything to him? I never knew that such minor information could expose such a shade of him. I don't take the call. A message immediately pops up:

If you don't take the call now, I will know for sure he is with you.

He video calls me the very next moment. My hands start shaking. The message sounded like a warning. And what did I do to deserve it? I was honest with him. I pick up the call. I see Raghav and he can see me. He asks me to show him around the place. *What has got into him?* I say no. He is adamant. I feel embarrassed. I do as I am told. He sees nobody. He starts saying something but I cut the call and switch my phone off. Trust isn't by nature foolproof. It is made foolproof by your belief in your partner. Today Raghav busted a myth for me. Till now, I was under the impression that he was one of those rare, liberal men and that I was fortunate to be with him. How liberal a person can be with his partner probably depends on how well he knows her and what he assumes about her. The difference between the two often breaks more relationships than love ever builds. I can't concentrate on work any more. Maybe it is obvious. Why else would my producer ask me to take a break? I don't say no. I go to my room and lie down on the bed, seething with anger and embarrassment. I know why exactly Raghav video called me. Not just to make sure that I was telling him the truth but also to make me feel guilty. And women and guilt go a long way. If not for guilt, I believe women could never have been controlled by men. Raghav tried to do the same with the video call. How can you meet your ex when you have a husband? That too in the middle of the night? An ideal woman should have not opened the door. An ideal woman who is married would not have met her ex-boyfriend, or some bullshit like that. Raghav is afraid that I might fall for Kshay again. What if we have sex? It could only mean that I chose him sexually over Raghav. Men and women are hardwired to perceive sex differently. For men seek a conquest in it and women, an experience. Is this why a man, subconsciously, seeks a different woman in his mind once he is done being physical with one woman far too many times? But a woman, more often than not, seeks that one phantasmal man of her dreams in the different men she goes to bed with? I decide not to feel guilty. Now when I close my eyes, I feel better.

A noise wakes me up. I don't know what happened. I check the time on my phone. Pretty late. I missed dinner. I check my phone again. Raghav has called a few times but, of course, I haven't picked up. He will conclude that I'm upset. Or that I'm with Kshay. His mind, his thoughts, his conclusions. I can't be blamed for it. I hear a sound outside my door. It sounds as if someone is scratching it. I feel scared but get up to open it. I find Kshay on his knees, struggling to get up. One look at his eyes and I know he is drunk. He is blabbering something which I can't understand. I help him up and he puts his arm around my waist. I don't know why this move of his makes me alert, makes the hair on the back of my neck stand up. Is it because Kshay and I share a physical history? Or is it because this touch is what Raghav has a problem with, or that I know just how he will react if he got to know about this. *If* he knows. It makes me feel like I'm ahead of Raghav. Like I can hurt him the way he hurt me this morning.

Kshay is continuously blabbering. I ask him to stop but he doesn't. I search his pockets and find the keys of his room. I open his room, switch on the lights and take him inside. Somehow I manage to push him on the bed. I cover him and switch off the lights. I have almost walked out of the room when I pause. I don't know what comes over me but I go back and kiss him on his lips. I quickly come back to my room. I lie in bed and stay awake the whole night.

* * *

Night Five

I've been forever impulsive. That's one thing I hate about myself. At times I do things without thinking. And then I dwell on them knowing fully well that they can't be undone.

The kiss was real. Best part though, I'm the only who knows about it. Kshay was too drunk. Raghav won't ever get a confession out of me again. Men don't deserve certain information. They can't handle it, no matter how much they claim they are cool with it. I feel thrilled: I know something that Raghav won't ever know. I like this feeling. Maybe kissing Kshay was impulsive, but it was provoked by Raghav. He made me feel wretched when I didn't do anything. When he asks for a video call next, I won't mind a bit.

Today is the most exciting day of our trip. We are going to trek to a place called Triund and camp there at night. I don't call up Raghav. I leave him a message saying I'm going for a trek with my team. If he wants, we can video call any time. He sends me a few kiss emoticons. I want to slap him but I understand my message has massaged his ego well. Marriage is just like a compass. We know which way we are heading, but it's impossible to know where exactly we are. We are always focused on, think and talk about where the future is. But never realize if we really know where the present is. This overlooked present becomes a shocking future later. I'm sure Raghav is unaware of what his chauvinist attitude has provoked me into doing. If and when he learns about it in the future, he will think that I'm the one who cheated on him. But he cheated on me first by breaking the code of trust. Why is it cheating only when one's spouse has stepped out of marriage? Why isn't it cheating when the code of trust between two people is violated? Why is sleeping with a third person a prerequisite for cheating? Raghav was never like this. That was why I had married him. But now I know this chauvinism was lying dormant in him. Whether he pretended to be liberal in front of me but wasn't really, I will never know. But I feel cheated. He isn't the husband I had married. So who is the bigger cheater? Raghav or me? Or both of us?

It is late by the time we reach Triund. But the trekking was one of the best experiences of my life. Our plan is to camp here all night and return in the morning. As we locate the place where we want to set up our camps, I notice one tent is already made. As my team begins to set up our tents, one at a time, I notice a man standing outside the already made tent and clicking a photograph of a mountain peak. I smile. I excuse myself and approach Kshay.

'You too were trekking?' I ask.

'Hey! Just what I had hoped for,' he answers with a warm smile.

'Don't tell me you still use hope and me together.'

'I don't.'

'Huh?'

'I use hope, you and me together. The best threesome one can imagine.' His warm smile now has a naughty hue.

'Yeah, sure. You never did that when we were together.'

'When we were together, we were together. What was there to hope for?' he says, looking at me directly. I feel as if the past four years were an illusion. As if they never existed. That's another peculiar thing about Kshay. Or perhaps about Kshay and me. We always seem to pick up where we left off effortlessly. We never have to start from the beginning. We are always in medias res.

'Are you seeing someone?' I ask. I had to.

'I think I am.'

'Just like you *thought* we were seeing each other. The truth being, of course, that I was trying to make it happen.'

'Just because our ways were different doesn't mean I didn't try.'

'Maybe you did. But our destinations were different. Hence, our trying processes were also different.'

'You wanted something contrary to my core.'

'Yes, I wanted to settle down with you. What else can a woman want from a man she is in love with?' This is something I have been asking myself since we decided to separate.

'You know what's the worst thing society does to us?'

I look at him expectantly.

'It makes us believe that there is no alternative to whatever it wants from us. It fucking convinces us that whatever it has designed over the centuries is an absolute. And the ones defying it are crazy people who deserve to be judged and shamed by one and all.'

He has a point. That's why I don't say anything. I get a call. It's Raghav.

'Husband?' Kshay asks. I nod.

'Tell him you are with me.'

I ignore him and tell Raghav I'm with my team, setting up our tents. I tell him I will call once we're done. Kshay is smirking. I shrug.

'That's another reason why I don't want to settle down with someone. I can't be brutally honest with her. Nobody can.'

He again has a point. I don't say anything. At that moment my director calls me. I don't tell Kshay anything. I go back to my team while he enters his tent. Later, we retire to our respective tents and I have some hot tomato soup from my flask. I make a short video call to Raghav and then cut the call saying I'm sleepy. There's a constant emotional itch in me to reach out to Kshay. He'll never let me be at peace with myself. He is that chaos which makes you feel that it would have been better not to have met him in the first place, but also makes you realize that had you not met him, you wouldn't have been what you are today. He made me connect to my ruins. Raghav made me connect to my will to make a house amidst those ruins, using the debris. And now Raghav has . . .

'I was thinking . . .' I hear a male voice. I sit up startled. It's Kshay.

'Sorry. I didn't mean to scare you but I had this new book with me. And I was thinking if you want to read it with me. The way we used to,' he says with a twinkle in his eyes. It tells me he misses the past as much as I do. It makes me feel relieved. *The way we used to* . . . Kshay is crazy about books. Every time he read a new book that he found unputdownable, we would cuddle up naked under a blanket. My head on his chest, his arm around my shoulders and him reading the book. I would listen to him and be lost for hours.

'What say?' he is waiting for an answer. If he knows me well, he should know my answer too.

* * *

Night Six

I keep looking at him. I feel a spell taking over me. I simply kneel down and begin to strip. Kshay zips up the door of the tent. I take off my woollens and my inners. I shiver but don't mind the cold too much. I'm distracted. His eyes travel down my body from my eyes to my lips to my breasts to my belly to below. I feel tempted to ask if there's any change. Do my breasts look as firm as they were when he touched them for the first time? Do I look as much in shape as he found me years ago? My train of thoughts stops as he begins to strip. The broad shoulders are still the same. The sparsely hairy chest. The perky nipples. The stretch marks. I always had a thing for his stretch marks. He pulls his underwear down too. I don't look at his penis. I keep my eyes firmly above his waist. Kshay takes out a book, probably the one he was talking about, from his jacket. He comes and gets inside the blanket. An unprecedented arousal grips me the moment our naked skin rubs against each other. He lies down. I place my head on his chest. We don't say a word but the way we move our bodies tells me nothing is over between us. Everything is still there. We only turned our emotional faces away from each another, and tried to pretend that everything was over. The comfort is both beautiful and disturbing. Perhaps it is disturbing because it's beautiful. A married woman isn't allowed to feel such beauty in another man's arms no matter how much peace she finds herself there. My husband changed my home from Kshay to him but there are certain addresses nobody can change for you. Kshay is one such address for me.

He begins to read. I know he is hard but I don't touch him there. He doesn't make any move either. I always admired this quality of his. Any man would have fucked me by now. He won't. Not until I want him to. Only then. That's also why I avoid looking at him. Sometimes you don't know what story your eyes hold. And how a man will interpret it. He keeps reading. I feel the urge to ask him if the scar on his back is still there. I feel the impulse to kiss every inch of his body. He keeps reading. And I'm lost in my thoughts. I don't know when we doze off.

In the morning I wake up hearing a man call my name. It's my director. The moment I realize I'm naked, I panic. I tell him I'll come out in a bit. He leaves. I look around. There's no Kshay. His book is there right beside his pillow. I heave a sigh of relief. I quickly get dressed and check my phone. Thankfully no calls or messages from Raghav yet. When I come out of the tent, I find that Kshay's tent is still there, but he is nowhere to be seen. My team wants to trek further up but they tell me we'll be back here for the night and finally go back to Dharamkot tomorrow morning. I like the idea. The book was dogeared at page 204, I remember checking it after I woke up. It's far from over.

It is nine in the night when we come back from our trek. It went smoothly. Others prepare a bonfire while I look for Kshay. He is sitting right outside his tent. He waves at me. I wave back. My team and I have dinner by the bonfire and sing old Hindi songs. Everybody gets drunk a bit and later retire to their tents. I prefer to stay next to the bonfire. Kshay approaches me. This time we exchange even fewer words. We go inside my tent and strip; this time lying closer to each other. The way he puts his arm around my shoulder, the way I place mine on his chest; the way I place my left leg on his groin, feel him getting harder; the way his body smells; everything speaks of our past more than the present moment. But visiting the past has repercussions. Sometimes I wonder if those repercussions are created by our own selves more than the situation. Kshay finishes reading the book. He turns to look at me.

'What?'

'Remember the game?' he asks. I know what he is talking about. In a flash he turns me over. He doodles something on my goose pimple-dotted skin using his warm tongue. I guess the word: love. This is a game we used to play before. He would scribble words on various parts of my body and I would have to guess them. Then I would do the same to him. Whoever guessed more won. I keep guessing every word he scribbles on my back, thighs, inner thighs, belly, shoulder, arms correctly. I stop him at the tenth word and do the same on his inner thighs. He guesses it wrong. I giggle. I do it on his balls. Wrong again. The moment I grab his erect penis, I don't scribble any more. I suck it. And till late in the night we make uninhibited and soul-exhaustive love as if Kshay and I are beyond the past, present or future. Beyond societal rules. Miles away from our own prejudices.

Next morning when I wake up Kshay is again gone. I check myself in the front camera of my phone. I look flushed. I blush.

* * *

Night Seven

My eyes open with a jerk. I realize my flight from Mumbai has landed in Delhi. I look around. My team members are looking outside. I realize it has happened again. I call it an emotional fantasy. I love to revel in the what-ifs of life. And all of them invariably involves Kshay.

I switch on my phone. Among other messages, Raghav's is the first one: *call me when you land. Love you.*

My husband is a sweetheart. In fact, he has successfully challenged what Kshay had made me believe about men. But for some reason Raghav is always a sneaky chauvinist in my fantasies. Is it because even in my fantasies, I need my husband to be unlikeable for *crossing lines*? Marriage is certainly about lines. But a line which is centred around a circle. Many keep moving around in that circle and some go ahead and cross it. Few are like me. We cross those lines, along with a validation, but only in fantasies. It's so funny. Maybe I'm too happy with Raghav, but not done with Kshay. So one side of me wants to live the fantasy, while the other side is very comfortable with Raghav and wouldn't want such a thing to happen in real life. I always have these fantasies when I'm travelling and not when I'm in Mumbai with Raghav.

From New Delhi, we reach Mcleod Ganj in a bus and then to Dharamkot, where we have an Airbnb house booked for us. Impulsively, I ask the owner of the house if the only other vacant room after we checked in has been taken. He says no. My director asks if I'm expecting anyone. I shake my head. In fantasies, you don't expect anything. That's why they are so much more idealistic than reality. And, of course, nobody judges you for anything. I go to my room and call up Raghav; I tell him I've reached. I grin when he says he wants to see me. A video call.

After a sumptuous dinner, we retire to our respective rooms. The recce begins tomorrow. I can't fall asleep. I think of calling up Raghav but it's too late. He has had a long day in office as well. He might not say it but he needs to sleep. I toss and turn in bed. The room is really cold and in spite of having covered myself with two thick blankets, I can still feel the chill.

There's a knock on the door. I sit up and check my phone. 12.45 a.m. *Who could it be at this hour?* There's another knock. I get out of bed with my phone in my hand. I can feel the coldness of the floor through my socks. I reach for the door.

'Who is it?' I ask.

'I'm sorry, but I was wondering if you have any spare cigarettes?' a man answers from the other side. I swallow nervously. Is it really happening? Or is it still a fantasy? The third knock is softer.

I open the door.

The Vacation

Alarm one: 5.30 a.m.

For a stranger who visits my house in posh New Alipore in south Kolkata, it won't take too long to know my name: Radhika. If he looks at the nameplate next to the door, he will know my full name too: Radhika Bose. Not just that. He will know exactly how many people stay in my house—eleven. A house where my name is on everyone's lips, especially in the mornings. At thirty-four, I'm the eldest daughter-in-law in the Bose household. I've an eight-year-old daughter, a loving husband, my in-laws, two younger brothers-in-law, their wives and their two children. I had an arranged marriage when I was twenty-two. My husband says I had reminded him of Maa Durga when he had seen me for the first time, because of my big, round, expressive eyes. I was happy to know that but I would have been happier if he had said that I had reminded him of Madonna.

Although I didn't understand it back then, after twelve years, I have understood one thing. My husband respects me a bit too much, which is great. I hope they make more men like my husband. But it is also true that where there is too much respect between two people, there's also an unbridgeable gap between them. Everything is perfect between my husband and me, and yet there's a lacuna. Everyone in my family loves me, and yet there is a feeling of, at the cost of sounding a little harsh, being imprisoned. Maybe because I was never the sort who wanted to be domesticated, but was forced to at a young age. A couple of years were spent getting used to my new role, and then Mini happened. Time flew and I didn't have time to ponder over anything else other than my family. Now that I have time, I wonder: why can't I too work like my friends? Why can't I be financially independent like them? I'm not blaming anyone. I just feel sorry for myself at times. I pity myself. I remember the time when I had told my husband that I wanted to join a gym. He had to talk to his parents for a month before I was allowed to go. I would leave home in a sari, change into my gym clothes, and then come back in a sari. The love, the respect is there . . . but I feel shackled ever since I stepped into this house as a newly-wed. I see my sisters-in-law and don't find them troubled by these chains of domesticity. Maybe they aren't aware of them; once you're aware of them, it gets increasingly difficult to live with them. But to live without them, is that too much to ask for?

I tried talking to my best friend from school about all this; she said I was being unrealistic. And selfish. She said some people just can't digest too much goodness. And that's what was happening to me. I agree there are people having a far worse time than me. But is that a reason to brush away this feeling that is gnawing at me? I think women are placed right at the centre of their family's equilibrium. Any unsanctioned, untoward act of theirs can disturb that equilibrium. And nobody is not ready for that. Sometimes we ourselves aren't ready for a change. But for the last three months, I have been readying myself for something. It won't disturb any equilibrium but will allow me to experience life in a different way.

Today when the alarm rang, I was already wide awake. I hadn't slept. Today I need to inform my husband (who will then inform everyone else) about my vacation. I'm leaving for New Delhi to visit a college friend, who is on her deathbed. Other friends of mine are also visiting her. I will be travelling alone for the first time since I got married. I will tell my family that I'm going there for two days, but will eventually extend the trip to seven days. I've rehearsed my lines a thousand times in my mind. The conviction with which I deliver them is what will make or break my plan. I can't afford the latter because it might break my life no end. I will be lying to him for the first time in twelve years. It's a big risk, I know. But just as the consequences of getting caught scares me, the sheer fact that I can possibly pull it all off excites me no end. After sending Mini to school and just before breakfast, when my husband is getting ready to go to work, I will inform him about the trip. I have a funny feeling in my stomach. It's not a normal vacation after all. It is a sexual vacation that I'm headed for. I take a deep breath, hold it for a few seconds and then exhale. I get up.

* * *

Alarm two: 10.30 p.m.

I cannot quite believe that I did it. My husband fell for my story hook, line, and sinker. He explained the situation to his parents and even they bought it. And now I'm on my way to New Delhi. My husband and daughter saw me off at the airport. My eyes were moist as I kissed Mini goodbye. I hoped that one day when she was a grown up and got to know the reason behind this vacation, she wouldn't quite comprehend it. As understanding it would mean that she too had undergone what I had. And I cannot wish such a future for my daughter even at the cost of being misunderstood by her.

This chain of events was set into motion the day I accepted the friend request of a man named Atulit on Facebook. There's nothing fancy about him. He is twenty-five; he was an engineer and is now taking a break to prepare for the civils. Last year he managed to crack the prelims but couldn't clear the mains. This year he is confident of cracking both. He hails from a small town in Bihar and lives alone in a spacious two-bedroom apartment in Gurugram. The house actually belongs to his uncle, who stays with his family in the US.

I don't know why we started chatting on Facebook messenger, exchanged numbers—I had to save his number under a woman's name—or why I decided to spend a week with him. Atulit is the real reason why I'm going to New Delhi. But maybe that's only partially true. The reason I'm on this flight is me.

As I drag my suitcase out of the arrivals gate, I nervously scan the crowd in front of me for Atulit. Although I had told him to not come pick me up, he had insisted. I find it weird to meet someone for the first time at an airport. I had gone to the washroom immediately after landing to make sure that I was looking my best. It doesn't take long to spot him. My heart is pounding. He waves at me. I had always assumed that I looked different from my pictures, but seeing that he recognized me almost immediately makes me feel that perhaps I was wrong. I wave back.

Although we had chatted about hugging each other, when we meet, it feels a little awkward. We settle for a handshake. My courage resurfaces in his car. A housewife who had lied to her in-laws and husband to travel to New Delhi to meet a man much younger than her. The thought itself gives me goose pimples. I pinch myself to believe that it is all real.

Atulit gently puts his hand on mine as we stop at a traffic signal. This touch is different from our handshake. It feels too good to be true. We entwine our fingers together. But soon have to let go as the signal turns green. My husband calls. I tell him I've taken a cab and am on my way to my friend's house. I share an awkward smile with Atulit after the call ends.

As he unlocks the door of his apartment, I feel a knot in my stomach. I know what is going to happen inside this house for the next seven days. I know there won't be any turning back once I step inside. My fantasy is slowly turning into reality.

Atulit is waiting for me to come in. So I step in hurriedly. I don't look around the place much. He asks me to sit on the sofa and goes to fetch me a glass of water. I take a deep breath. I suddenly long for my husband, my daughter, my in-laws, my comfort zone. Am I really doing something wrong? Ask anyone and the answer will be a vehement yes.

'You must be tired. Why don't you sleep tonight? The other bedroom is for you. Let us talk tomorrow morning,' he says. I'm glad that he is turning out to be the same person that he sounded like in our chats. I nod and go to the bedroom. It is nicely done but looks as if nobody has lived in it for a long time. I change in the washroom, lock the bedroom door and try to sleep. I think of calling my husband when my phone's alarm rings. It is 10.30 p.m. It is time for my father-in-law to take his blood sugar medicine. I'm the one who reminds him about it every day.

* * *

Alarm three: 9 a.m.

The last time I woke up at nine in the morning was when I used to be in college. I feel happy; I'm living in the moment after a long time. I have lived as a wife, a mother, a daughter-in-law, but never for myself, in the moment. Every morning so far I have woken up and worried about breakfast. Once that is done, the daily chores have to be taken care of, then lunch, Mini's homework, snacks for my in-laws during tea in the evenings, and finally dinner. And mind you, this is not a one-day thing. This is my schedule seven days a week and for 365 days a year. So much so that I have become so used to planning ahead that right now I am finding it difficult to be in the moment. In the moment . . . in Gurugram, in Atulit's apartment . . . in a strange bed far from my own . . . Am I really here?

I pick up my phone. There is no call or message from my husband. I'd told him that I would be staying with my friends and would keep him updated. He hadn't asked any questions. Either he trusts me a little too much or he thinks he knows me a bit too much. Or maybe he takes me so much for granted that he finds the idea of my cheating on him ludicrous and impossible. He used to be possessive of me after our marriage. But after Mini was born, his possessiveness dimmed. Maybe he let his guard down as he felt I could no longer be attractive to anyone any more? As if being a wife robs a woman of her desires and being a mother robs her of her will. A husband demands your absolute sacrifice. A child needs your absolute surrender. Between the two, so many thousand desires die a silent death.

I hear a knock. I get out of bed and open the door.

'Good morning.' Atulit has a tray in his hand. He has brought breakfast: sausages, poached eggs, bacon and a pot of coffee. I remember telling him how much I love an English breakfast. He remembered. I suddenly feel wanted.

'Did you sleep well, Sayesha?' he asks as he places the tray on the side table.

I am Sayesha Sen on Facebook. Although my profile picture has my photo, I deliberately chose a different name. My family, my husband's family, cousins, colleagues, everyone is there on Facebook. I wanted to break free from the people I already knew in my life and connect to strangers by being myself. Had I not had this urge, I would never have met Atulit. I don't correct him. I prefer the lie to stay a lie. I intend to deactivate my Facebook account once I go back home, change my phone number and erase my digital footprints, almost as good as never existing.

'Yes, I did.'

'This is for you,' he says with a heart-warming smile.

'I don't have anything before brushing my teeth,' I tell him with an amused smile.

He keeps looking at me for some time and his smile grows wider. 'Remember?'

I know what he has on his mind. He'd told me that he had a thing for morning smooches. The raw, stale-breath smooch. I'd told him I didn't have any such fascination. Now standing in front of him, I realize I had told him so because whatever we had chatted—or rather sexted, as it is called—was done assuming that none of it would come true. Atulit comes closer. He is a good five inches taller than me. He is lean, but feels strong when he holds my arm with both his hands. I gulp nervously. I feel like a prey. And within the four walls of this room, where nobody knows we are there, that feeling has a disturbing arousal associated with it.

'I'm sure you won't mind changing your rules for once,' he whispers as he leans forward to kiss me. We kiss till my jaws ache. What happens in the next two hours is still a daze for me. I do everything most unlikely of me.

I bite, scratch, moan loudly, allow myself to be taken in positions I've never been in before. I feel liberated, aware of my body, of myself. It is when I finally collapse beside him after riding him for the longest time that I understand why this is so unlike me. Not because I'd never imagined myself doing all this but because I had never done them before. After all these years, I've realized that I was never sexually content with my husband. I always feared his reaction if I moaned a little louder, if I told him I enjoyed dirty sex? I could never be thoroughly honest with him. I understood that when you live with someone every day, exposing your dirty side to that person is not always easy. Unless there is an assurance that he won't see you only in that light. In my case there has been no such assurance to date.

* * *

Alarm four: 4 p.m.

It struck me last morning when Atulit and I had prolonged toe-curling, stomach-churning and emotionally draining sex. I had an arranged marriage. I didn't know my husband well enough before getting into bed with him. There was an undeniable restraint in me, which he negated with a subtle force from his side. I think it was necessary else I wouldn't have been able to do anything at all. Was I comfortable?

That's a different story. Although unknowingly, but it happened differently with Atulit. We chatted and at times talked over the phone. By the time I met him, I felt that I knew him. This knowledge produced a certain comfort during our sexual tryst the previous morning.

We always judge people on the basis of their sexual preferences and practices in spite of knowing that emotions are all that matters. I didn't fly to Gurugram for sex. If it was only about sex, I could have done it in Kolkata itself and nobody would've ever known. This vacation was intended for other purposes: to believe that I can still be desired by someone other than my husband, that there is more to life than my family, that I'm not a victim of nuptial attachments, that I can live a different life without upsetting the equilibrium associated with my roles as a wife, mother, daughter-in-law.

I managed to help Mini complete her homework via a video call. I updated my husband last night about my fake friend's health status, asked him about everyone at home. Even though I lied, I didn't compromise my duties. And I feel good about it. Honestly, I had my doubts about Atulit. Had he come across as predatory, I would have left immediately. But thankfully he wasn't anything like that.

We had dinner at this lovely Burmese restaurant called Burma Burma in Cyber Hub. He is quite chatty, which I like. I know he is trying to impress me. I've also distinguished a hint of awe in the way he looks at me; he is chivalrous and gives utmost importance to my comfort. I feel so damn alive. Sometimes I think that a little attention and care are we all need. But I know for sure that if our dalliance stretches beyond a week, Atulit's adoration will start fading. And he too might turn into my husband. How I wish we can forever remain elusive to our domestic partners. But then I also know that that's the essence of a domestic relationship: the mundane and the monotonous. We are all emotional explorers deep inside. Some are easy to pacify and some aren't. For the last twelve years I had been itching for an exploration and I'm happy that I'm having it now.

We went for a movie and then had lunch at his favourite restaurant in Connaught Place. He wanted to take selfies but when I told him that pictures make me uncomfortable, he didn't insist. He wanted to shop for me as well but I was strict. I couldn't allow him to do that. Maybe he doesn't know that I flew to New Delhi not for him, but for myself. I won't blame him if he interprets my visit as something that I'm doing for us. By the time this ends he will hate me forever. I know it. And still I am okay. For once I'm being selfish. If that's the price I have to pay for being myself, for once, I guess I'm okay with it.

We came back to Gurugram. Atulit wanted to take me to an amusement park. But I reminded him that I'll have to be at his flat.

The alarm beeps. It's time to go on a video call with Mini. I need to finish her homework. I can sense Atulit's irritation, but he says, 'After that whatever I say. Okay?'

I smile and nod.

I'll be back to this reality in a few hours, I tell myself.

* * *

Alarm five: 9 p.m.

For over forty hours, we haven't left the apartment. I've been the centre of his attention. It feels so good to mean something to someone, even if it is just for a day or a week. I feel like a word which kept wondering about its existence till it read its meaning in the dictionary. Atulit, for now, is my dictionary, where I read about different meanings of myself. It's funny how different people help you realize different meanings of yourself. My husband, at the beginning of our marriage, had a completely different meaning, or idea, of me. He was always trying to be mischievous with me. I enjoyed it too. But I don't know when it simply ebbed away. Nowadays, we go without sex for months without even telling each other, 'Listen, we should do it. It has been long.'

Relationships are like a bag full of gifts. The moment we get it we are excited to open it. But after we find out what the gifts are, the excitement fades. My husband

and I are past the initial, exciting stage. But with Atulit, I've only just started. In between our love making, I look at him and smile to myself. He once asked me to leave my family and be with him. He is so naïve. He really thinks it is that easy to leave everything. He actually thinks I'm with him because I'm done with my family. No! This isn't a runaway scenario. Nor is it an escapist module. This is just a vacation. And vacations are meant to be temporary. They are meant to rejuvenate you. Perhaps prepare you well so you can take on the monotony of life again. But I don't tell Atulit anything. I keep nodding whenever he talks about our future. I only make sure I am not misleading him with false hope and fake promises.

We are sitting on the floor under the shower in his bathroom. He is behind me. We are cuddling. Atulit is saying something. I barely listen to him. I only keep caressing his hand. He is too young. He is yet to understand the importance of silence between two people and the romance behind it. No words, no touch, no sight except for the realization that the person you want to be with is there beside you. I've tried to experience it so many times with my husband, but his silence is different. His silence never acknowledges my presence.

Now, we are on his balcony. He is smoking a cigarette and sipping his beer. I'm happy with my ginger tea. I took three–four days to get used to my new environment.

Initially I felt as if I was sleepwalking through everything. Someone would wake me up and I would realize that I was only dreaming. But since last night I've slowly become more conscious of my new reality. Maybe because I can sense that the end of the vacation is near. I'm trying to live every moment as much as possible. I only wish that Atulit was a little bit more mature. Not that I would have extended my vacation if he was. But just that when a surfer goes to ride the waves, he doesn't wish for smaller ones, although riding even those will give him an adrenaline rush, but the bigger ones will become a part of his story. Atulit will never be a part of my story. I know this for a fact. Since I didn't really have any expectations from this visit, I'm not disappointed. With every slipping second, I wonder if I will ever again have the guts to pull off a vacation like this in my life. I guess not. So many things need to fall in place for that. I notice that Atulit is looking at me. He is done with his beer.

He comes close, places his hand around my waist. I'm used to his touch now. He draws me closer and kisses me. It turns into a slurpy smooch. I taste his beer, he tastes my coffee. I'm almost lost when I hear the alarm. They are a part of my story. The greatest gift of my married life: a constant awareness of time. Atulit starts kissing more passionately but I wriggle out of his embrace. After all, it's time to call my husband. I need to inform him that my friend, who never existed, breathed her last. And I shall be home the day after.

* * *

Alarm six: 8.45 p.m.

Today is the last day of my vacation. I'd thought I wouldn't sleep last night. But after we made out, I slept like a log for a long time. Atulit is clearly feeling forlorn. Seeing a man not being able to handle separation turns me on. I haven't ever witnessed it. Not when I am the subject of his troubled dilemma.

'Stay,' he pleads. I say nothing and kiss his forehead. A kiss is always a loaded expression. The way we kiss someone contains so much more than long passionate speeches. If one can feel it properly and truly then there won't be any questions and answers in its wake. No misunderstandings either. This makes me wonder when I had kissed someone so passionately before. My husband and I would usually kiss before having sex. That kind of kiss is different. It only speaks of hunger. This one is different. It is emotional, pacifying. And just when I thought Atulit can't surprise me any more, he tells me that since it is my last day, he wants to take care of me.

'What do you mean?' I ask.

'I want to bathe you. Dress you. Cook for you. Make you feel like a princess.'

A part of me wants to crack up laughing because I'm not used to such jokes. Another part of me wants to break into tears because I know it isn't a joke. Nobody has ever *done* such things for me. Why am I so special for him? I'm tempted to ask but I don't. Sometimes it is better to not know the answer. I tell him he can do whatever he wants to for me, with me.

He takes me to the bathroom and makes me sit on the bathroom dice. He wets my hair and applies some shampoo. The way he massages my scalp is deeply arousing. Or maybe it's the care. We women are so much about the process. I close my eyes and savour the moment. After he is done shampooing me, Atulit soaps me. I look at him transfixed. This is better than I had imagined. This, by far, is the best part of my vacation. It has the best balance of sensuality and emotions, which is what I was seeking when I came to Delhi. He turns me around but instead of soaping my back, he holds me tightly.

'I've never had a woman like you, ever,' he whispers in my ears. Does he know when a man makes a woman realize she is exclusive, special, not something random, what it can do to a woman? Uncompromised attention and emotional pampering is what we seek all the time.

He wipes me with a towel, helps me slip into a bathrobe. As I step out of the bathroom, a towel wrapped around my head, he asks me to make my next demand. Unknowingly, he is making sure I miss this vacation. I tell him I want to have something Chinese for lunch. He orders the food. When it arrives, he feeds me. And I have been the one feeding people all these years. The sudden role reversal is both exhilarating and pleasantly embarrassing. Why did I have to find a guy on Facebook to deserve this? Why didn't my husband do this for me? Why don't I ever feel this desired at home? I feel choked but don't make it obvious. I excuse myself and go to my room.

It's evening. Atulit has come to drop me off at the airport. The last six days seem to have flown past. He is holding my hand. Sometimes tightly; sometimes gently. We reach the departures gate. I turn to look at him. I know my eyes are moist. What I don't know is if it's because my trip has come to an end or if I can ever take such a trip again.

'Why are you crying? We shall meet soon. If you don't come here, I'll come to Kolkata. Any which way we are meeting,' he says.

NO, we won't. Ever. Only I know this. I don't tell him that. He kisses my hand. I kiss him on his cheeks. And without any further delay, I let go of his hand and walk in through the sliding doors. I turn to look at him. He waves at me. I have a lump in my throat, identifying the same hope in his eyes as I had on the first night of my marriage.

44

While collecting the boarding pass, the alarm rings. I call my husband and tell him I'm about to board soon. I deactivate my Facebook account before my flight takes off. Once I land, I break my phone, the SIM card, throw them in the dustbin. And walk out of the Kolkata airport. Only for me, it feels as if I'm waking up from a beautiful dream. But now I don't know why I feel like I'm cheating on Atulit more than my husband.

* * *

Alarm seven: 5.30 a.m.

Radhika.

It feels nice to hear my real name after a week. Everyone is happy I'm home. They don't have to rely on themselves any more. I'm also happy I'm home. I don't have to rely on others for my own happiness any more. Last week is enough for me to sit down in solitude and spend the rest of my life reminiscing about it. I know I will go through everything that happened again and again and again in my mind, making different versions—good and bad. Sometimes smiling to myself, at times feeling choked. For the world, if it ever came to know, I will be called unfaithful. But for myself, I am a woman who did what she wanted to do, for the first and the last time, without disturbing any equilibrium.

It feels funny to get into the same routine after a week's break. I feel a renewed energy in me. For my family, I have come back after bidding goodbye to a dear college friend. But my demeanour tells them otherwise. Not that anyone has confronted me about it, but probably they'd expected a sad Radhika to have arrived from New Delhi. They are not to be blamed. How do I explain it to them that I needed this one week to know whether I was still the one I thought I was? I'm ready to confess everything to my husband but will he ever understand that whatever I did was not to cheat on him?

I had missed Mini the most. I hugged her tight, feeling emotional, for a few seconds. She will soon grow up and get married. But I will never want her to undergo an emotional stasis. But maybe it is inevitable. I'm sure my mother must also have experienced it. The only difference between her and me is that I decided to do something to end that period. I broke the monotony of my domestic life. I may no longer be as interesting to my husband, but I felt the thrill of being desired and admired by someone much younger. And my life is certainly not mundane. I went on a trip that very few will ever undertake in their lives, scared to create creases in their otherwise smooth lives.

My husband comes home from office in the evening. I have prepared his favourite dish for dinner. He gives me a box. It is a new phone. And a new SIM card registered on his name this time. The first thing I do after switching the phone on is set the alarm at 5.30 a.m. From tomorrow onwards I will be Radhika Bose again. The one my family knows. The one I know as well.

Tomorrow Is Cloudy

Minute One

R orders a vegetable puff and a cup of coffee at the Costa Coffee outlet across the boarding gates at Indira Gandhi International Airport, New Delhi. It's 5 a.m. R has been at the airport for seven hours now. Her flight to Mumbai was scheduled at 11 p.m. last night but due to inclement weather conditions—there was too much smog and visibility had dropped to zero—it has been delayed. Her husband had advised her against travelling during such a time but that didn't stop her from making the trip.

R waits for her food to arrive, yawning every now and then. After a long time, she had stayed up all night. A Costa staffer places a tray in front of her and leaves. She picks up her cup of coffee and notices that all the nearby chairs are empty. She chooses the one closest to her. She takes her time sliding into the chair. In her second trimester now, she is finally getting used to her changing body than she was in her first. She tears open the ketchup sachet with her teeth at one go. It reminds her of someone who had always told her that she had really sharp teeth. But instead of sachets, she'd be nibbling and biting that someone's skin. The thought squeezes out an impulsive faint smile. As if it had all happened yesterday.

R bites into her puff and takes a sip of the coffee. She looks around. There's a smoking zone adjacent to the food court. R has somehow managed to stay away from cigarettes since she got pregnant. Her husband and her in-laws don't know that she used to be a smoker. As her gaze travels from one person to another in the smoking room, it finally comes to a stop on one man. Only his side profile is visible. That's enough for her to know who he is. She feels a thud in her heart. She stops chewing the puff.

* * *

N slept more than he thought he would. He slept through the alarm that he had set for 3.30 a.m. It was only when his wife called him at 4.30 to find out if he was ready to leave the hotel that he woke up. In the next fifteen minutes, he freshened up, checked out of the hotel, and took a cab to the Delhi airport. He had to catch a flight to Hyderabad. He took out his cigarette packet after clearing the security check. Empty. He threw it in a nearby dustbin, located a counter where he bought his brand: Marlboro. It was while he was waiting for the shop boy to give him change for Rs 2000 that a woman came up to the counter; she asked for a Davidoff. It reminded him of someone. A nostalgic smile lit up his face. He had once played a kinky game with a cigarette of that brand. One cigarette, two people, each allowed to take puffs alternately. Whoever finished the cigarette first got to sexually enslave the other for a whole day. The moments, the puffs, that someone . . . everything flashed in front of him. Certain memories never fade. He took the change and headed towards the smoking room. Before entering, he got himself a coffee from Costa Coffee.

There weren't too many people in the smoking room. N lit his cigarette and took long puffs, exhaling gently. Flying out on weekends had become a routine since he had taken up the latest project in his office. It was exhausting. Flights, hotel rooms, boardrooms, meetings . . . life had never been this monotonous.

N was about to stub out his cigarette when he found a person staring at him from outside the smoking room. From across the stained glass doors, the woman's features were blurred but there was no mistaking her. Hot ash from the cigarette fell on his finger. It hurt but he didn't flick it away. It had been ten years since he had last seen her, since they had sworn never to see each other again.

* * *

Minute Two (R)

The moment our eyes meet, I look down. But I am immediately seized by the desire to look up at him. To see if he is still looking at me. That would mean he had recognized me. I was hungry a minute ago but I feel suddenly full now. I put the puff down on the tray and pick up the coffee instead. Reflexively, I look up at him. He's still staring at me. I know that look. If only looks were letters, I could decode each and every word of that look.

I feel slightly nervous. I didn't know I'd feel so when I'd see him next. I place the mug on the table, get up and leave. As I pass by the smoking room, I find him shuffling out. I pray he doesn't call me. I had planned to pretend not to recognize him if I ever ran into him. But one look at me and he will know everything. He always knew where to fish for my secrets—in my eyes.

Dragging the Samsonite along with me, I briskly walk towards my boarding gate. I have a strong urge to turn and see if he's following me. If he is, I want to know if he has been trying to seek me within him all these years.

I check my boarding pass; five minutes are left for boarding to start.

Although it has been a decade since we last saw each other, I have imagined this situation a hundred times.

What if we bumped into each other? Every time I had the same answer: so what? I will pretend not to remember him. Now I realize that this pretence won't work. It's for the world. But with one's self, only unadulterated honesty works. But such honesty has more questions than answers. For example, how do you insulate yourself against the best memories that you've had with a person whom you can't have? But then having him within is also having him, right? Just like we retain the moral of a story heard in kindergarten throughout our lives, we keep the thoughts of a person we loved forever. People without thoughts are only bodies. And mere bodies don't make any context. They are like words that can't do anything without a context. Within one, they seem magical. Anyone can play with words. But not everyone has stories. N and I were stories.

Actually, I never really let go of N. Never really forgot him to not be able to remember him after a decade. He was always there in my heart, alive and alongside every event of my life.

I feel a little tired. I must tell this to my gynaecologist in my next visit. I have been feeling tired more and more frequently these days. I reach my gate, sit down and place my Samsonite next to me. From my vantage point, I can see him approaching me. I pray that we aren't on the same flight. His slow gait makes me wonder: certain vulnerabilities shouldn't be granted wings. For they fly you to a place called chaos.

* * *

Minute Three (N)

I look at my watch. I fail to remember if it's day or night. She hasn't changed much. I remember her well. She has put on some weight. So have I. She wears specs now. So do I. She has changed her hairstyle. I sport a stubble now. She looks like a woman now. She was too much of a girl back then. I too was a boy. The similar changes make me feel as if we were together apart. I remember I have half an hour before the boarding starts. I stub out the cigarette and leave the smoking room. By the time I reach the Costa Coffee counter, I see R walking towards the boarding gates. I notice the half-eaten food on her tray and wonder if I should read more into it than required. If it's a signal? Follow me; don't follow me? Too cryptic. I leave for my boarding gate as well. She may think I'm following her but I'm not. All right, maybe I am. I check my watch again.

I remember telling her once that what a soul is to a body, time is to a clock. And we were about the time and not the clock. I forgot the context of that line but I remember her looking deep into my eyes and saying nothing on earth could take her away from me. We separated a few months later. But she was right. I've revisited our story many times after our break up. Over the years, I got convinced that if we were in a relationship now we would never have separated. It was a mutual decision, and yet I keep going back to it, correcting the mistakes, smoothening the edges, perfecting it. I've a wife now and a two-year-old child. I love them. But what I had with R seems more alluring in hindsight. Maybe because I didn't live it completely like I'm living the life with my wife and kid.

I can easily walk past her but I don't want to. I can approach her and exchange pleasantries, engage in friendly banter. I won't. I just want time to slow down. I don't know when I will see her again. Just the mere sight of her has jolted me. If someone had told us about this future encounter ten years ago when we were together, we'd have probably said that we would sneak out and make out like two animals in heat in an elevator or something. And now I'm afraid to make eye contact with her again. We were two wild birds once, who could fly high together but never make a nest. We were each other's choices but always whined about each other's preferences, lifestyles, dressing sense, etc. I don't know which is more painful: the fact that we didn't survive or that we survived fine without each other. It makes me wonder about the frivolity of promises in a relationship. When I was in it, towards the end especially, everything felt like a punishment. Years later,

I find that experience educative. I want to know if she is happier without me. The memories of our days together sometimes poke me like thorns when I unconsciously reach out for them. Is she happy teaching me not to believe in something wholeheartedly since everything—just about everything, doesn't matter how promising, beautiful and in control—runs the risk of getting completely destroyed?

I notice her sit down. I understand that she is pregnant. She looks up at me. I want to but I can't take my eyes off of her. Should I smile? Or just stare?

* * *

Minute Four (R)

Our eyes are linked. Is it a game already? Who will deflect the gaze first? I don't. He doesn't either. He is standing at some distance from me. His eyes had contained a raging fire once upon a time . . . I want to know if that fire is still on. Maybe it is still there but I can't feel it any more. Earlier I would get burned in its intensity. And that was the ultimate pleasure. To burn in a fire fanned by the one you love. A point where lust and love diffused into one and you couldn't distinguish one from another except for focusing on the innate pleasure that it gave you. I never felt it with my husband.

It's not that I never loved my husband. I couldn't love him. Not after N. I felt as if I had been emotionally

55

hijacked. Then I started hating N. I felt like a puppet in the hands of his memories. I started feeling as if I didn't have any control over myself, or my heart. To compensate for the lack of passion, I became extra dutiful towards my husband. I didn't give him a chance to complain, neither as a wife nor as a person. I didn't become meek but rather more adaptable, adjusting. A quality I didn't have earlier, which is what had led to our break up. Should I tell N that I'm finally the person he always wanted me to be? There's a lump in my throat.

All these years, I had a vague, apprehensive feeling of having lost something. But I couldn't quite figure out what it was that I had lost. Tonight I know. I lost our love story. It remained unfinished. Had we not had a history, our gaze might have lingered on each other for a tad bit longer— strangers who caught each other's fancy in a half-deserted airport in the wee hours of the morning. But we share a past, our story is not complete.

N was there the night I conceived my first baby but neither he nor my husband will ever get to know this. The pregnancy was unplanned. My husband and I were on a houseboat in Kerala. I intuitively knew that I would get pregnant that night. And I wanted nothing more than N to be there where I took on the role of a mother. I also wanted him to be the cause of this change and he was on my mind during the act. From the time my husband penetrated me as I closed my eyes till he was done and I opened my eyes,

N was there within me. I cried myself to sleep after we were done, thinking I would finally be someone he didn't know. I have a lump in my throat now and my eyes are moist. But I won't rub them. He might guess that I'm crying. And I don't want that. Tears are dangerous. Tears give people, especially the ones who had been the reason for them, a chance to see your soul naked. And that's the one nudity you feel more scared of than shyness.

I am distracted by a call. It's my husband. My hand begins to shake. I suddenly feel guilty looking at his name flashing on my phone. As if I've been caught red-handed doing something sinful. I take the call and ask him to wait for two seconds. I stand up, turn my back to N and shift to another seat, tugging my Samsonite along.

* * *

Minute Five (N)

I wish she hadn't received that phone call. Was it her husband? Is that why she stood up and turned her back to me? R was always like that. She spoke in gestures when overwhelmed. But does that mean that right now she is . . .

Why did we meet each other when we were young? Too young. When we wanted to be in a relationship but couldn't handle it, sustain it. I was too possessive; she was too wild. She was patronizing; I was egotistic. I feel we were right for each other but weren't ready at that time.

With time, I've realized that too many lies in a relationship stales it while too much honesty kills it. R and I were too honest with each other. We were too frank, often at the cost of wounding each other beyond healing. Honesty mixed with maturity is important. We were difficult. For her, it was okay to meet boys but if I met girls, she would feel insecure and start fighting with me. It was always about what she wanted. If I so much as told her not to flirt with other boys, I was accused of curtailing her freedom. It cannot always be my way or the highway in a relationship.

And I think everyone will agree that the mere pressure of sustaining an already stressful relationship can at times prove to be too demanding. The year before we broke up, I feel, we stayed with each other simply for the sake of it, because we didn't want to let ourselves down, after all we were in it forever, weren't we? *Ours will last a lifetime and beyond* . . . and all that jazz. It took us a year to realize that not everything was meant to last a lifetime.

Too much closeness and intimacy ends up making a relationship stifling and not transparent, which is the desired result. This observation is based on my relationship with R. Perhaps that's the reason why I've never been too close or too distant with my wife. I love her. But our relationship is not stifling, maybe because I haven't bared my soul to her, not let her into my core. It makes me wonder if my wife knows that behind our successful marriage is a woman named R. And the lessons I've derived from being in a relationship with her.

Sometimes I feel R was my childhood, my adolescence, while my wife is my adulthood. One applies the lessons learnt in one's early years throughout adulthood. I'm a different person now with my wife. Do different people make you behave differently? Probably. I'm so tempted to know how R is with her husband. Is she as wild with him as she was with me? Or has she been domesticated? How would we have fared as a married couple? These questions mar my present, never letting me see the past the way it was.

R is now sitting closer to a boarding gate. She is done with her phone call. If that's her boarding gate, then I'm afraid we are heading towards the same destination. I smirk at the thought of this. Were we ever heading towards the same destination? We had only taken a road that was common. We had only experienced a journey together. But then roads end, journeys don't. Somewhere, somehow it continues, lingers on. We can't do anything to stop it. It may fade, but is never erased completely. Like R had faded for me until I spotted her tonight and suddenly everything resurfaced in vivid details.

I have an overwhelming impulse to strike a conversation with her. If she says she is not interested, I will back off.

But the way she was looking at me tells me otherwise. People are queuing up in front of the boarding gate close to her. I start walking towards her.

* * *

Minute Six (R)

What is marriage but an emotional straitjacket? When you wear it, you also clamp on a set on societal blinders along with it and sign away any agency to loosen it. The day I or my husband takes off this straitjacket, we'll be done.

I have never told my husband about N. I have wanted to and he did ask me once if I had had anyone in the past but I simply shrugged it off and told him it hadn't been serious. I don't think my husband would have understood what N and I had shared. There were multiple shades in our relationship. Sometimes we couldn't get enough of each other's bodies while sometimes we were content to share silence and a smoke together. Sometimes the two were mixed up. I have never had such moments with my husband. But I don't doubt that he hasn't experienced them. Maybe with someone else? Maybe he too has agonized over the death of a relationship? Maybe he too is vulnerable. Maybe he too was imagining someone else's face in his hands the night we conceived our child. These maybes sustain our relationship.

Sometimes I feel like an ignorant teenager, wishing to run away from every responsibility and into N's arms, into a life that we did not lead. I smile. I think like this because N and I were never about responsibilities. We were there. That's it. We owed nothing to each other. Except for some intense emotional moments. A thought suddenly occurs to me. What if I approach N and ask him if we can fly away somewhere together? I find that I've broken into a sweat. I admonish myself: what am I even thinking? But I can't help but have these thoughts. Will he accede to my request? If he does then will it at all be a request? It will be . . . well, I can ask him that much, right?

I bend to take out my water bottle from the bag and gulp down all the water at one go. I feel restless. He must be married. Maybe has a kid as well? How could I be thinking of going away somewhere with him like that in gay abandon? I have a husband. A baby in my womb. I should be the one rejecting such an idea instead of nurturing it. Can't I temporarily switch to a different life, be with different people, in a different environment? But nobody is allowed such an abrupt change. No one is ever free.

I turn back to find him coming towards me. My throat goes dry and my heart starts thumping loudly. And when he is right there in front of me, it stops.

* * *

Minute Seven

R stands up as N approaches her. She struggles a bit; N asks her to be careful. He almost touches her but withdraws his hand at the last moment. Good for him. Better for her. Finally, they stand facing the other. Has so much time really gone by? His salt-and-pepper stubble confirms it for her. The faint reddish tinge in the parting of her hair confirms it for him.

'Congratulations!' N blurts out.

For a moment, R can't wrap her head around the context of the word. Why would he say something like that? They are meeting after a decade. Then she realizes it's for the belly.

'Thank you.'

'Which month?'

'Fifth.'

N gives a tight-lipped smile. R smiles awkwardly as well. Although they have so much to say to each other, not a single word comes out of their mouths. Their thoughts are all over to be phrased properly into coherent, polite sentences.

'So . . .' he says.

'So?' she asks.

'How is life?' he asks.

She had never thought that their relationship would ultimately boil down to the dregs of small talk.

'Good,' she says, nodding her head a little. 'How is yours?'

'Good.'

'Where are you heading?' he asks, trying to keep the conversation going at any cost.

Before she can stop herself, R blurts out, 'I don't know.'

'Sorry?'

'I'm sorry. Mumbai. I'm heading to Mumbai,' she adds quickly.

'Oh! I'm flying to Hyderabad.'

'Work?'

'Home. Delhi was work,' he says. The last word knocks the wind out of her. 'Home'. She had never thought that he would ever mention this word and she wouldn't be a part of it.

'Mumbai is my home now,' she says.

'I guessed.'

A few quiet seconds later, she asks, 'Are you married?'

He flashes a quick smile, which she can't decode, and says, 'She is an amazing cook, takes care of me; she is a working woman, never lets me question whatever we share . . .'

R smirks. 'I get it.'

'You do?' N is surprised.

'But you never liked monotony.'

He takes his time to respond. 'Now I live with it. I loved a lot of things earlier that I don't live with any more. Our definition of home changes over time.'

'Do you know the best and the worst thing about these *homes*?'

'You tell me the best. I'll tell you the worst.'

'They shelter us from each other. I can say no to one only because I have another.'

'And the worst is since they were made by us, though for different people, they still call out to us. Especially after midnight, when others are asleep. When our soul is most awake. Waiting for a call perhaps.'

There is an announcement; boarding for R's flight has started.

'I have to go now,' she tells N.

You'll never be able to go, don't you get it? N thinks.

'Sure,' he says.

R joins the queue. N doesn't move from his spot. He would have loved to kiss her once. She would have loved to hug him once. But they both know it would only have stirred the dust that had settled over the years.

N is waiting for her to walk out of the boarding gate. There are four people ahead of R. An airline staffer comes and tells her that old people and pregnant women can jump the queue. R follows her. She stops, turns around and comes back to N.

'Will you kiss my belly?' R is at her most vulnerable self now, pleading in front of him. N feels choked up. Seconds later he kneels down and kisses her belly. *You don't know how lucky you are*, he whispers to her baby and stands up. She looks at him longingly. Then she leaves.

I'll shrug off this encounter the way I shrugged off my past when my husband had asked me about it.

R's last thoughts before she wears her spectacles and shows her boarding pass to the airline staffer.

Our ashes may smell of the same story in the end but what the fire of life burnt down in us will be two different things. You and I, we were different and so we couldn't make it. We were different so we will always crave for that what if. N's last thoughts as he watches R go past the boarding gate and disappear into the foggy dawn.

Clicks

Day One

Everything in my life is right. But nothing seems correct. I understood the difference when I was meeting with a prospective match, who is now my fiancée.

I wasn't ready for the engagement. But I didn't know how to stall it. I'm thirty-two, good-looking, and the vice-president of a successful start-up. Except for 'I'm not ready' I had nothing else to say to my parents. And that wasn't a good enough reason for them. Not after using it for the past four years. You'll be ready the moment you marry, they told me. But they never really understood me, not now, not when I was sixteen and wanted to study humanities and not the sciences.

I'd been having an existential crisis. I felt that I had ticked off everything there was on the list of a successful life. A high-end corporate job? Done. An SUV? Done. A property? Done. Trips abroad? Done. Marriage? About to happen. A perfect life on social media? Yes. But were these all there was to life? What was the meaning behind having and doing all these things? What was I actually doing with my life? Did these things ultimately matter? My life was so predictable. Everything was exactly how it was supposed to be, and yet I felt nothing. I barely felt alive. As I said, everything was right. Nothing was correct.

And just when I was starting to feel a little hopeful, a little excited, the proposal came along. Last month I had bought a DSLR—Canon 500D—on a whim. As I watched one YouTube video after another on its usage, read photography manuals for beginners, the whole art seemed alluring. It produced the same eagerness to learn in me as cricket had when I was a kid. I was passionate about the sport like nothing else in my life. That is until I bought the Canon 500D. There was finally something to look forward to. Framing, light, focus, shutter speed—these words would keep reverberating in my head even during office meetings. I would be itching to go back home, make a peg of Jack Daniel's, pick up my camera and start my next experiment. *My* Canon 500D. I hadn't been this possessive about anything or anyone in a long time.

Photography gave me a chance to escape my otherwise monotonous world. People say photography isn't about capturing a subject but about capturing light. It has made me feel that life isn't just about tangible things but also about your feelings. And that is precisely why I have taken a week off from work. It is monsoon here in Mumbai. And it's time to put my theoretical knowledge on photography into action.

It's Monday. After an indulgent breakfast, I drive straight from my apartment in Andheri, Lokhandwala, to Sanjay Gandhi National Park in Borivali. Nothing is more magical than trudging through muddy tracks in the wilderness on a rainy day. On the way, I smirk when I see people scurrying to their offices.

I take as many photographs as I can in the national park. With every click, I smile. I'm delighted to discover that I can still connect to something so deeply. How many of us can say that once we have grown up? There is no pressure under which I click. I don't have to prepare a pie-chart of my photographs. They are beyond the brackets of success or failure. The last time I had done something with such gay abandon was in kindergarten when I had learnt to draw an apple for the first time. Everything I have done after that, in one way or another, has been about beating someone else or my own self.

It starts raining harder. I dash inside my car. I check my photographs in the meantime. Zooming in, making sure all parameters were followed. I clean my lenses and then decide to drive to Bandstand. I want to capture the sea and the Mumbai city line.

It is drizzling now. I have bought a cup of coffee at a cafe near Bandstand. I take out my zoom lens. This lens makes me feel like everything is within my reach, magnifying details I'd have normally missed. I mount it and then pick up the camera; close an eye and peer into the viewfinder, adjusting the lens. Before clicking the city line, I take a random photo to check if everything is in order. A couple sitting in a cafe across the street. And magnify it to check. The cafe looks warm and mellow, its lights twinkling merrily on an otherwise grey day. The couple is sitting near the window, their outlines blurred by the raindrops on the glass. The man looks dapper; he is clean-shaven and wearing rimless spectacles. The woman—my lips part a little and I frown—is my fiancée Shrutika. When I had last called her, she had told me that she would be busy in office all day.

* * *

Day Two

What I saw yesterday is with me today. They left an hour later. I left an hour and two minutes later. While driving back home, I realized there were two Shrutikas. I was engaged to one and the other I knew nothing about, except that she had lied to me. A most terrible revelation about a person one is just getting to know. Especially if it is your betrothed.

To date I've had two major relationships. One was long distance; it started after I graduated. It lasted for four years till the girl got married to someone else. Then I dated a colleague from my second workplace. We were together for five years. But she didn't think I was very involved in the relationship; I was too 'detached' for her. She called it off. I knew she was right. I've always been a detached person in all my relationships—romantic and familial.

Since we have got engaged, Shrutika and I call each other every night. In the beginning, the conversations were fresh; now they have a pattern. She tells me how her day went. I tell her about mine. What's in store for the next day; maybe we could go for a movie in the weekend; try out a new restaurant after the movie, etc. She sometimes sends me screenshots of *lehenga*s she would like to wear on our wedding day. We are yet to tell each other 'I love you'. Or give kisses over the phone. We have held hands whenever we have met outside, but nothing intimate has happened till now.

Last night after talking to her, I opened the snap and looked at her and the man. Was he her ex-boyfriend? What was she doing meeting him after lying to me? There was a time during the phone call when I was tempted to ask her why she had lied. That I had seen her with a man in a cafe, but I chose not to tell her anything. I didn't want to sound controlling or possessive. Maybe she will herself tell me later when she was comfortable. I never probe people to tell me anything. But I'm also incorrigibly curious.

Today, I went to Marine Drive and clicked a lot of photographs. But I kept glancing at my watch more than peering into the viewfinder. I was waiting for them. I went to Bandstand again and stood on the road across the cafe where I had spotted them yesterday. There they were: Shrutika and that man. I mounted the zoom lens and clicked twenty-five photographs of them. I felt like a detective. Why did I do it? I don't know. They left after an hour. I left after two hours. Not before checking every picture that I had clicked. *Did my photos expose a story she was trying to hide or was my mind scratching a surface beneath which nothing lay?* I didn't have an answer.

* * *

Day Three

After toying with my camera all morning I've come to Bandstand after lunch. My parents think I am exploring Mumbai in the monsoons. I did tell Shrutika I'm on a week-long holiday, but she never asked me where I had been, the places I had visited or about the photos I had clicked. I too didn't tell her anything. I never tell anyone anything about myself if they come across as uninterested. So it's only me who knows I've come here not because I want to click photos but . . . I don't remember the last time I had done something without knowing why I had done it. I'm not usually like this. But then I can be whimsical too at times.

I order a cappuccino and wait for them, rather impatiently. I start going through previous photographs of theirs. I try to understand the man. I feel it will help me understand the relationship they share. Especially his glasses. They are rimless. I remember Shrutika telling me once to change my glasses. I have black carbon framed ones. Maybe she wanted me to get rimless glasses like this man. He is clean shaven while I have moustache. Maybe she doesn't like moustaches. She could have just told me that straightaway. But then I too haven't asked her anything directly. All that I have been able to think in the past two days is the story of Shrutika and this man.

On an impulse, I call her. I sense the surprise in her voice. Has she already taken me for granted? Has she already told the other man, 'Oh, I know my would-be very well'? I'm here in this cafe because I don't know her that well. If I had not taken a week off, not bought the DSLR, would I have ever discovered this daily rendezvous?

I ask myself what my real problem is: finding my fiancée with a man or the fact that she has been hiding these meetings from me? Why hadn't she told me about this man? Didn't she factor in the fact that I might get hurt if I found out the truth? But I realize that it's actually my ego. I feel offended.

It stops raining. I check my watch. There's time. I walk into the other cafe and take a seat in their usual spot. I look across the road to the cafe, outside which I'm usually stationed, spying on them. What will Shrutika think if she saw me there? Will she wave at me? Will she hurriedly leave, pretending not to have seen me? Or will she confront me—something I will definitely not do? I get up and go back to the other cafe.

I click a few shots of the city line, the grey clouds, a few birds, a puddle, a mother walking with her kids, but nothing gives me satisfaction. I wonder if they have decided to meet elsewhere. The thought disappoints me. I was hoping to find out a little more about their story. A picture is worth a thousand words. I check their photos again. I compare them with Shrutika's and mine on my phone. We look formal, they don't. We seem slightly caged, they seem free. They were yet to touch each other in my photos and yet exuded a mysterious chemistry. Their smiles are warm towards each other. Ours lack any essence. There was a basic difference in their togetherness and ours: time. Time's a prerequisite for anything to blossom. The pages of their journey were already filled. Ours were still blank. They were limited in that sense. Their story must have already traversed a certain path. Ours was still looking for the correct one.

There is another basic difference. We are supposed to get married. Not them. Three hours and four cups of coffee later, Shrutika and the man are yet to arrive.

* * *

Day Four

Our lives are all about patterns. Either we create them ourselves or slip into already established ones. Maybe we find solace in them. I'm yet to meet a person who is happy and has no visible pattern to his life. But there can't be happiness without any pattern. Pattern and monotony are different. And jumping from one pattern to another isn't easy. Life is most interesting when we are in between two patterns. When we are trying to let go of one and struggling to embrace another. Like I am steadily letting go of my bachelorhood and trying to get used to a pre-marital life.

I realized this when Shrutika, during our daily nightly phone call, made a most unusual request. 'Can we have lunch together?' We have never had lunch together on a weekday!

Shrutika told me, on our way to the restaurant, that she had found the place on Zomato. It was in Juhu and was called Melting Pot; the place had got favourable reviews. I replied with a non-committal 'hmm'.

'We should meet during weekdays too. What do you think?' Shrutika asked after we had ordered our food.

'Yes, why not?' I replied. She smiled as if she had known I'd agree. But what tormented me was why she had made such a proposal now? Why today? That's when I thought about patterns. As the waiter served us the food, I wondered if marriage was the most involuntary pattern that we got into.

We bantered about nothing in particular while having lunch. What was funny was that I was the one who was on leave but was glancing more frequently at my watch than her. As if I wanted her to be in that cafe at Bandstand more than I wanted her to be in Melting Pot.

Shrutika surprised me by kissing me on my cheeks as we got inside the car. When I tried to kiss her back, she deliberately puckered up her lips and we smooched. After that, we grew quiet. First the lunch, then the smooch . . . two unusual events one after another. Was it because she was feeling guilty? I thought about a friend who always got a gift for his wife whenever he fucked his colleague. Sometimes an expression of extra love is triggered by guilt, he had told me once. Was Shrutika guilty about meeting the man without telling me?

She requested me to drop her off at her office. I wasn't surprised. I'm mostly chivalrous so I got out of the car to bid her goodbye. She hugged me. It was a tad longer than our previous hugs. I think that we usually hug a person longer than usual when we aren't sure that words will do justice to what we have on our minds. Some feelings are indescribable. I wonder what Shrutika was trying to tell me through this longer hug.

I told her I was going home but instead drove to the cafe in Bandstand. And waited for them. As I took my usual seat, the waiter approached my table and asked, 'Cappuccino with no cream, right, sir?'

Even the cafe and I shared a pattern. I nodded with a smile. An hour after their usual arrival time, the man walked into the other cafe. The smooch made sense now. He loitered around for some time and then got a call. He sat alone in their usual spot and kept looking at his watch. I understood he was waiting for her. Half an hour later, he simply left. I kept waiting. Shrutika didn't arrive. I suddenly felt like I had won a war without even picking up a sword.

* * *

Day Five

From the time I've woken up, I've been feeling relaxed. The sky is murkier since last night but there have been no showers yet. I don't think I will go to Bandstand today. It has been some time since I indulged with my camera. I decide to go to Fort instead and take photos of people. The business district of Mumbai offers an interesting confluence of eighteenth-century British architecture and modern, twenty-first-century officegoers. It is an ideal site for any amateur photographer. Or for a professional for that matter.

I drive there, click a lot of photographs, but as it nears lunchtime, I have an urge to go to Bandstand. I try diverting my mind by focusing on different subjects—a beggar, a sleeping taxi driver, a man waiting for a bus, a cobbler. Then my phone rings. It's Shrutika. She asks me where I am and then tells me she has some work outside office. After disconnecting the call, I drive to Bandstand. They aren't here yet although it is well beyond their usual meeting time. This time I enter the same cafe that they frequent and occupy a seat outside. That is when I notice the man. He is sitting inside, next to an air conditioner. Beside him is a bag. Shrutika's bag. And the chair is pulled out. My instinct says she must be in the washroom. I cancel my order and leave hurriedly. I walk across the street to the cafe that I usually visit.

As I settle down, I see them traipsing out of the cafe. My heart starts racing. I feel a vein throbbing in my head. It suddenly starts pouring. Typical of Mumbai rains. People run helter-skelter, dashing into shops or under their awnings. The man with Shrutika opens an umbrella. It obstructs my view. I can't see them clearly. And when you can't see something properly, you start assuming things. And usually assume the worst.

I am certain that she met me yesterday because she was feeling guilty. Did Shrutika think: I'm going to kiss this man but I also want to convince myself that I like my fiancé? The thought is silly because, surely, she couldn't be kissing this man for the first time? Or maybe she is kissing him for the first time since we got engaged. I can't think clearly any more. My thoughts are as blurred as my view. The skies take mercy on me. The rain stops as unexpectedly as it had started. My eyes are fixed on the umbrella. Till the man closes it. Their proximity burns a hole in me. My heart tells me to confront them but my mind asks me to sit tight. The thing is I don't want to catch them red-handed. I don't want to pronounce my presence between them. It makes me wonder when such a triangle is formed, who is between whom? Am I in between both of them? Is he in between Shrutika and me? They must have known each other for a long time. That answers who is in between. And it angers me. I stand up reflexively. The table wobbles and my phone falls down. I pick it up; sit down and call up Shrutika. If I know I'm the one in between them, then they should know it as well. I find her staring at her phone. She walks away from the man a little. *She knows I'm in between.* Why is she taking so long to pick up? Guilt again? I'm convinced she won't pick up. But she does. Almost at the last ring. I'm at Bandstand today, I say, clicking photographs. And as I tell her so, I balance the phone between my left ear and shoulder and pick up my camera. I can only hear her breathing.

* * *

Day Six

Shrutika thinks I have a good sense of humour. She told me this last night. As I eat my breakfast today, I can't help but smirk. The look of panic, helplessness and alarm on her face when I told her that I was in Bandstand was worth it. She looked around frantically trying to locate me. But unlike her, I had my zoom lens. I saw her every movement. It cracked me up. Laughing, I told her I was joking. She visibly relaxed after that. That's when she told me I had a good sense of humour. Seeing her getting worked up was arousing. Somewhere, I understood my importance in her life. I can cause a storm within her if I wanted to. I had never had such control on anyone before. I don't think she would have got so worked up if instead of me it was the man who had called her up. That's the power of a *husband*. Or would-be husband to be precise.

Marriage, for the first time, made sense to me. Now I'm convinced that marriage too is a power game. And if my hunch is right, she won't ever meet the man on Bandstand again. One call and I've pushed them into changing their meeting place. I've also understood something about myself. Most men in my position would have confronted her already. That's a much more masculine reaction than being a mere spectator of these secret meetings. But I've always felt uneasy with certain expectations that are attached with being a man. And if one doesn't live up to those expectations, one's masculinity is supposedly challenged. Just like women, men too are prisoners of societal shackles.

Anyway, let me not digress. Others may have done what they wanted to but I didn't confront Shrutika. I won't. After a long time, I have something that makes me wonder, which has incited my curiosity. At nights, I analyse their possible story, and at daytime, I try to second guess what could happen. It's almost like I'm the author and they are my characters. If I don't like the fact that they meet in Bandstand, one call and I've rewritten their rendezvous location. But speaking of Bandstand, I wonder where they will meet today, or if at all they will.

Today being Saturday, Shrutika has an off. I drive to her house a few hours after breakfast. She stays with her parents in Santa Cruz, west. It's a cooperative society. I park my car across the main gate of her building. It's pouring like crazy today. I call her. We talk for some time. She tells me it is a lazy day and that she will sleep it out. I tell her I'll do the same. I think she was curious to know what I would do today, the same as me. She doesn't know it but we are in a game. Relationships are like that, aren't they? Even after ending the call, I stay where I am. I have a hunch that she will step outside soon. She does. A little after lunch. I don't know why she always chooses this time. Maybe it's convenient for the man.

It's drizzling now. A few minutes later, around 2.30 p.m., an Ola cab stops in front of her building. Shrutika gets inside. I follow the cab. *Bandstand?* I wonder. In a few minutes, I understand that she isn't going there. *Somewhere else*, I'm sure. After forty minutes, the cab goes inside the premises of a posh society in Khar, west. Half a minute later, it comes out. There's no Shrutika in it. I stay parked outside. *Is this where the man stays? Will they meet at his place from now onwards?* It's a bad thought. If they are or were in a relationship, they must have met in there so many times. I choose to wait. But this awaiting is different than the one in the cafe at Bandstand. I get impatient and anxious. There, I would usually be waiting for them to arrive. Here, I know they must have already met in the flat and . . .

I somehow manage to spend the next couple of hours. Shrutika has not come out. Curiosity gets the better of me so I get out of the car and go inside. I enter the society so confidently that the guards don't stop me for identification or to find out where I'm going. But once inside, I realize I don't know where to look for her. There are four buildings and I don't know which one she is in. It is not possible for me to find out without asking the guards, who can be nosy. It is when I'm in two minds that I spot Shrutika come out of one of the buildings. The man is behind her and is accompanied by a woman who is holding the hand of a child. They are all wearing raincoats. Quickly, I run for cover into the nearest building. Suddenly I feel the power has shifted from me to her. Although Shrutika is unaware of it. Good for me.

* * *

Day Seven

Shrutika sounded happy after she came out of that building. I understood this when she called me minutes after leaving the place in a cab. I was still on the premises of the building, although I lied to her that I was out on an evening walk. I couldn't fathom the reason behind her happiness? Who was the other woman? And the child? As I lay in bed that night, I thought that they must have been the man's family. But why would he introduce her to them? And they looked so comfortable with each other. The two women, I mean. I don't think I could ever be that comfortable with the man. Nor he with me. I didn't sleep well because I couldn't understand what must have happened between the man, Shrutika and the other woman. Did he tell his wife that he was having an affair with Shrutika? What about this news could have made his wife so amicable towards Shrutika?

In the morning, my mother told me that she had invited Shrutika and her family for dinner. I feigned happiness upon hearing it, but didn't actually want to see her. I had been racking my brains trying to understand Shrutika and that man's relationship and didn't want to come across as distracted when she arrived at home in the night.

They reached at five minutes past eight. After exchanging pleasantries, the elders stayed back in the living room while Shrutika and I went to the balcony. She sat on a bamboo swing while I stood against the railings. She told me she liked this spot the best in my house. I told her me too. We are not talkers. Often our silences are interspersed with a few questions from her and a few from me. I tried to read between the lines, hoping to discover something new about the man, but was disappointed. Our parents called us when dinner was ready. I tried to go back before her, but found Shrutika holding my hand.

'Give us two minutes,' she yelled and then looked at me. I shrugged. She had never held my hand like that.

'I need to tell you something,' she said. I immediately stiffened. I knew what she was going to tell me. I had imagined this moment many a time in the past one week. And lots of variations of it as well. But I had never imagined my throat going dry when the moment actually arrived. *I need to tell you something*, only a man can tell you how disturbingly threatening it sounds when it comes from his woman. Especially when he knows that she has been with another man.

'Sure.' I thought I sounded confident, but I was actually meek.

'I wasn't sure if I would ever tell you this,' Shrutika began. 'But something happened yesterday, and I thought there is a reason why I should tell you about it. We are getting married. I know we don't know much about each other. Of course, we will discover more over time but today I want to tell you about a man.'

There was a shrill ringing in my ears and her voice drowned. It died after a few seconds and I heard Shrutika say, 'We've known each other for the past five years now. We were in the same office. Now he works elsewhere. Although we met as colleagues, we connected as friends. I won't be lying if I tell you that he is the man with whom I have felt the most connected. He is a really good person. Incidentally, the year we met was the also the year he married his childhood sweetheart. They had a kid two years later.' She paused. *Come to the point*, I snapped at her in my head but said nothing.

'But then there was a problem. His wife started having an affair. So my friend went off the radar for a while and suddenly resurfaced a week before our engagement. In a pretty devastated state.'

And that's when you guys started having this affair, I completed the story in my head.

'I couldn't see him like that. It also made me think a lot about love and marriage. We are always taught that they are one and the same thing. But I realized they aren't. We don't know each other but are getting married. We might call it love if we are at peace in each other's presence. But I think it's more of an acceptance than love, isn't it?'

I got agitated. Maybe because I knew what she had on her mind but instead of telling me directly was beating around the bush.

'Maybe. So, what are you trying to say?' I asked her impatiently.

'My friend had caught his childhood sweetheart with another man,' Shrutika stood up. She was still holding my hand.

'I talk to him. Almost daily. More so in the last one week. And then I had a talk with his wife as well. She apologized, while I convinced him to give it another chance. But that's not why I'm telling you all this.'

As it still didn't go the way I had it on my mind, I spoke with obvious irritation.

'Then why are you telling me all this, Shrutika?'

'We will get married in a few months. I want you to promise me that if ever there's another woman, you will let me know. We won't catch each other. We will confess. Catch or confess . . . that is what makes or breaks a marriage, isn't it? Will you promise me this, Eklavya?'

I didn't know what to say. This was not what I had expected. I was ready for her confession. And for not some profound take on marriage. I must say I was a little disappointed. Her mother called again. This time a little impatiently. I used it as an opportunity to let go off her hand and hurried inside.

Minutes later, we were sitting opposite each other. In between dinner, I took out my phone and texted her: *I promise*. Looking at her I wondered what I was thinking. Sometimes we dwell too much on some things; we live our relationship so much in our heads that we end up pushing away our reality. And if your partner and you aren't a part of each other's realities, every other reason to be in the relationship becomes meaningless.

I looked at her. Our eyes met. Suddenly, everything seemed right. And correct too.

The Whore and the Wife

12 a.m.

This isn't her first time in the room of a five-star hotel. But it's the first time that she is free by midnight on a working day. Her code name is Meera. She is a luxury prostitute. Her real age is thirty-two while her professional age is twenty-seven. Her vitals are 34D–28–36. She has a rich café-au-lait complexion and high cheekbones, which put her in high demand. She charges Rs 2,00,000 a night. She gets Rs 50,000 in hand. She tends to five customers a month. She studied English literature in college. Any more information and you will judge her. Let her be a whore for now.

Tonight Meera's customer is a Gujarati businessman. Names aren't disclosed to her, but she could easily tell thanks to his thick accent. The man received a few phone calls, which further confirmed her hunch that he was a businessman. Meera is always on the lookout for interesting clients. She loves to guess about their lives, cultivating them in her mind. Perhaps it helps produce a sense of belonging. How else does one become someone's sexual slave for a night? The answer is simple: different people, different ways, but the method remains the same: use the mind to escape from what's happening around and with you. Till you get used to it. Meera wasn't up for it.but it is work and it's worship. She found herself in luck when her middle-aged, half-bald, potbellied, lecherous-looking client passed out in two minutes. She couldn't believe it. He had money but he didn't seem to have any class. She wanted to sip the red wine that she had ordered for herself; he had told her that she could order anything she wanted. But before she could finish her drink, he was stripping her. Then he stripped himself. The sight of him made her wish that she was drunk. He penetrated her wearing a condom. And the next moment he was done. Before he could even say anything, the man was snoring. Meera was thrilled. The super posh suite was now hers except for the naked businessman lying on the bed.

Meera took a hot shower, taking her time soaping and shampooing herself. She eventually came out wearing a bathrobe and a towel wrapped around her head and drew the curtains of the suite. Mumbai was spread out below, a glittering criss-cross of roads and buildings. The city was an everyday tug-of-war between dream and reality. That's what Meera loved the most about Mumbai. One simply couldn't guess which side was winning. Or losing. And then one day the sudden realization of victory. Or defeat. She slid into a chair next to the study table in the room, spread her legs on the bed and took her time finishing her wine. She wished all her clients were like the Gujarati businessman. She was even ready to charge less. Of course, she will not be allowed to. Her pimp was waiting for her in his car downstairs in the parking lot; he will escort her out in the morning. He was also there if things went out of hand. She could call him and inform him that she was done for the night. But she chose to stay in the room. Except for the guttural snoring, the night stretched out in front of Meera, still and unperturbed.

She put on some music on her phone and started dancing. She believed dancing to be the best form of expression. She looked at herself in the full-length mirror and clicked a few selfies. But stopped when she heard a sound, a beep. Three more shrill beeps followed. She turned towards the bedside table. Meera understood that it was her client's phone. On an impulse, she tip-toed to the table and picked up the phone. It wasn't password protected. She glanced at her client. He looked dead. Meera stared at the mobile screen. And two seconds before the screen light went off, she tapped on the WhatsApp message.

Are you there? I know you must be with some whore. I've always known this. Please tell me. Are you there?

She looked at the sender's name: wife. She was online. Meera didn't know why she did it but she texted back from her client's phone.

Yes, I am.

* * *

1 a.m.

Wife: I know you're probably thinking why I'm not calling you, right?

Meera (from her client's phone): Maybe.

Wife: When have I ever called you? And when, in those rare occasions that I did, have you ever picked up? In fact, I can't believe you are responding tonight.

Meera: I'm free. What is it?

Wife: Why, didn't you get any whore tonight?

No response from Meera.

Wife: You are surprised, right? How do I know? Well, a wife always knows. I've known for some time now. You opt for paid sex during your business tours.

Meera: Why are you telling me this now? Maybe I don't enjoy it with you any more, that is why I go for paid sex.

Wife: I read your credit card statement once. I understood there's always someone else with you in the hotels when you are away.

Meera: So why tell me all this now? Why not when you had read the statement?

Wife: You know how much I respect you. I would never be able to even think of such a thing about you. But then when I checked again and again, every time you travelled, I was certain. Some characterless woman must have manipulated you. I know it.

Meera (smirks): Oh! You already know she's characterless?

Wife: Which respectable woman sells her body for money? Or lures men from respectable families into such filth?

Meera (impulsive): I have a family too!

Wife: Of course, I know you do. But that woman doesn't, I'm sure. All she wants and knows is money and lust. This time when you come back, I've arranged for a small puja at home. It will weaken the spell of this woman.

Meera: Spell?

Wife: My Baba*ji* told me that women like these, who trade their bodies for money, know black magic.

Meera laughs out loud. Then checks herself; she does not want to wake up her client. This is turning out to be more entertaining than she thought it would.

Meera: You watch too much television, isn't it?

Wife: Only after completing all my duties as a wife and a mother. Why do you ask? I didn't know you had a problem with me watching television.

Meera: I don't. You should watch whatever you want to. And let me do whatever I want to.

Wife: I wouldn't have a problem if you did it willingly but a witch has cast a spell on you. She is trying to snatch you from me.

Meera: Which witch?

Wife: The woman who stays with you in the hotels.

Meera frowns at the message.

Meera: You haven't even met the woman and you are being so judgemental about her. That too being a woman yourself?

Wife: There is a difference between her and me. I'm a wife and I belong to my husband. She belongs to nobody. All she cares for is money.

Meera: Maybe she too has a family. Maybe she too is a wife, a daughter, a sister. Maybe a mother even, who knows.

Wife: I really feel bad for her family then. They will die of shame if they ever knew what she was up to. See, she doesn't even think of her family. What will she think of you and me? She is a home-wrecker.

Meera: We talk about men being chauvinists but women like you are worse.

Wife: Why would you say that? Have I done anything to upset you? You can tell me.

Meera: Have you ever thought that it could also be because he doesn't enjoy doing it with you any more?

Seconds later she sends a correction.

Meera: I mean I don't enjoy doing it with you.

Meera hurls the phone on the bed. She is furious. A few seconds later there is a beep.

* * *

2 a.m.

Meera thought she was done with what started off as mischief. When she texted back the businessman's wife, she was going to delete all the messages before she left. But now the wife had given her something to ponder over. It wasn't what she had told her; she had heard these things before. But they had never come from a woman. And it irked her. A woman is supposed to understand another woman. Did not the wife understand one basic thing: no woman sells her body as Plan A in her life? It's a plan forced on her by men and the society. The phone beeped again. Out of sheer curiosity, mixed with anger, Meera picked it up.

Wife: I know that you don't enjoy having sex with me. I'm at fault here. I know I've gone out of shape. I tried to do some medical tests too without telling you (I'm sorry) and I've been diagnosed with thyroid. I don't think I'll be able to bring my weight down much. But I'm trying. I starve myself these days.

Meera: Are you out of your mind? You are starving yourself to earn a man's validation? That too when you have thyroid?

Wife: Not for any man. Only for you, my husband.

Meera: The way you put it, it seems your husband belongs to some other species.

Wife: No! Please don't take offence. I didn't mean it that way. What I meant was you are my husband and you'll forever remain special to me no matter what.

Meera: Even if I go to a whore?

Wife: The whore is to be blamed. That's what I've been telling you. I know, given a chance, you will leave her but her spell is such.

Meera: She has a name. Meera. And she knows no black magic. I called her. She didn't call me.

Wife: You will never understand it. It's the spell.

Meera (having an urge to fling the phone away): That's forthright stupid. You know that, right?

Wife: I'll be patient with you. Babaji told me you won't agree with me. It may cause a fight. And that too is what the witch wants.

Meera: Why would she want a fight between you and me?

Wife: She wants to take my place. The whore wants to become the wife.

Meera: Just like you have sorted your 'husband' into a different category, you've done so with a 'whore'.

Wife: I know they too are women; but they are a disgrace.

Meera: Really? What do you know about these so-called black magic practising whores?

Wife: That they steal husbands and wreck homes.

Meera: They have their own husbands. And all they care about are their own homes.

Wife: They do? Meera has a husband? A home?

Meera: Yes. She has a husband. He tried to sell her off after marrying her to some sheikh in Dubai. She somehow managed to run off when, unknown to anyone, she was two months pregnant. Her daughter is four now. After tending to her clients, she goes back home. And guess what she does there?

Wife: What?

Meera: Narrates a fairy tale to her daughter. A new fairy tale every day. She is her daughter's emotional insulation from the world outside that is infested with wolves. But what's her insulation?

Wife: I'm feeling bad for Meera now. I can almost imagine her daughter's innocent face.

Meera (moist eyes): She is a fighter. She will sail through the turbulent times. You know the funniest thing about us is we never understand our inner strength when we have too many options in life. It's only when there are no options, no Plan B, nothing to fall back on, is when we realize how strong we are.

Wife: But why be a whore? Can't she do something respectable? What will her daughter think of her when she finds out in a few years?

Meera: All Meera cares about right now is how well she can bring her daughter up. Give her a good education and make her financially independent. If a so-called immoral cause is producing good results then what's the problem?

Wife: Hmm. Still . . . a whore?

Meera: Body, sex, money. These are the three vertexes of the social Bermuda Triangle that consumes everyone sooner or later. All she hopes for is before her daughter learns about her vocation, she should learn about the ways of society. Then she would be able to see that there's dignity in selling one's body for money rather than being some man's doormat.

Meera: Do you think to keep a soul cleansed when the body is being toyed with all the time is easy? Is it a joke? Can anybody do that?

Wife: I'm really happy I texted you tonight. You have made me see something in a completely different light. But now I have only have one question. May I?

Meera: Sure.

Wife: You did help me find respect for a whore, but why are you taking her side?

An emotional Meera suddenly stifles a giggle even as her eyes are still moist.

* * *

3 a.m.

Wife: What happened? Did I say anything wrong? I'm sorry if you felt bad.

Meera: I'm not taking anyone's side. I'm just telling you what I know about Meera and girls like her.

Wife: I'm sorry again.

Meera: Tell me something, why are you so meek? Why do you keep apologizing?

Wife: You are my husband. I need to be apologetic in case I say anything that hurts you.

Meera: That goes for everyone. If anyone says anything hurtful, he or she should be apologetic. But what is this you-are-my-husband thing that are you mentioning?

Wife: Well, my mother was always meek in front of my father. She rarely did anything that could upset him. But one day, she forgot to add sugar in my father's tea. To this day, the hair on the back of my neck stands up when I remember how badly he would beat her in front of my siblings and me.

Meera: Did you do anything about it?

Wife: I gave her medicines to soothe the pain from the beating.

Meera: But you couldn't hold your father by the collar and dare him to hit your mother again?

Wife: How could I? He was my father after all.

Meera: Meera had beaten her father with a stick once. Never again did he beat her mother or her sisters after drinking.

Wife: Would you have liked it if I had slapped my father?

Meera: That's the point. You don't need my validation or anyone else's for that matter to take a stand. If you feel that something is wrong, you should speak up. Else men like your father will keep defining our space and roles for us all the time.

Wife: Hahaha! You say 'these men' as if you aren't one.

Meera: I was just going with the flow. And don't laugh. I'm serious.

Wife: I'm sorry.

Meera: Again sorry?

Wife: I feel blessed to have such a husband who is so accepting of his wife's feelings. I hope I'm not dreaming about this chat. Don't get me wrong, but I've never seen this side of yours in all the time that we have been together.

Meera: We will come to 'how blessed you are to have me' later. But now I want to know why you didn't study? Financial problems?

Wife: Financial problems? You know my family. Do you think we ever had any financial problem? Girls in my family aren't allowed to study after class X. They say education ruins a young girl's mind. In fact, I remember you were happy that I was just a matriculate.

Meera: It's okay. I was a pig then.

Wife: Oh! Don't say such things about yourself. I respect you.

Meera: That is because your mind is trained to iron out all my creases.

Wife: Wait a minute. Our youngest has just woken up. I will text you after putting her back to sleep. Please don't go. I really want this to go on.

Meera: Take care of her. I'm here. Text me when you're free.

Wife: Yes. May I call . . . ?

Meera: No, texting is fine.

Wife: As you say.

* * *

4 a.m.

The client stirs in his sleep. Meera prays he doesn't wake up. She is relieved to see him turn over in his sleep. The snoring continues. The very next second the phone beeps.

Wife: Are you there?

Meera: Yes. The kid has gone back to sleep?

Wife: Yes. She's asleep. Maybe she was having a nightmare; she was crying out loud.

Meera: You are a good person.

Wife: I take it as the best compliment in my life.

Meera: Why, if I hadn't said it, it wouldn't have been true?

Wife: A wife's duty is to remain in her husband's good books always. So this is special.

Meera: Who taught you all this?

Wife: Nobody. I just know these things.

Meera: Hmm.

Wife: ?

Meera: Tell me if I, your husband, had not been there in your life, what would you have done?

Wife: I would have been dead by now.

Meera: Aargh! Can you just for one night stop acting like a doormat? You are an individual! Not

103

someone's pet. Your husband is just your husband, not your owner.

Wife: I don't know what to say.

Meera: Say 'I'm not anyone's pet'.

Wife: You are not anyone's pet.

Meera: Dammit! I mean 'YOU aren't anyone's pet'.

Wife: I'm not anyone's pet.

Meera: Better. And remember that always.

Wife: Even when you order me to do things that I don't like?

Meera: Like?

Wife: All right, I don't know how you will react to this . . . but now that we are chatting I want to be honest. I don't like it when you invite your friends home for drinking, and order me in front of them to serve snacks and prepare the drinks. I've cried in my room every time you've made me do it. Didn't you see how your friends ogled at me?

Meera: This is what I've been trying to tell you. It's no use crying. You should have slapped me in front of my friends the very first time I did that. Humans only understand the language of the cane. Especially those in a wolf's skin. Like me.

Wife: But you have given me so much as well.

Meera: All right, coming back to what I just asked you. Imagine a scenario where I am not there in your life. Suppose you had never got married. Then?

Wife: I thought about it. I think I would have studied further and secured a job for myself. I wouldn't have liked to be a burden on my father all my life.

Meera: I like that. For the first time, I've seen a glimmer of independence in you.

Wife: I always wanted to earn. I feel so happy to see the women in banks and other offices. I imagine myself in their place.

Meera: Then why don't you?

Wife: I have always feared how you would react if I . . .

Meera: The irony of the biggest manmade institution, marriage, is that a wife should rather hide her desires from her husband, fearing a backlash than tell him about them. And it is a bond for seven lives? *Bounded*, rather, for seven lives.

Wife: While reading your last message a question occurred to me. May I ask?

Meera: You don't need my permission. Not for this or for anything.

Wife: Thank you. I'm still getting used to this side of yours. Usually, you're so different . . . In fact, the very fact that we are chatting is surprising. Has Meera got anything to do with this change?

Meera: Maybe.

Wife: Why couldn't I do it? That too being a wife . . . Why couldn't I change you?

Meera: Maybe I haven't changed totally. Maybe Meera only ignited a spark. The fire has to be started by the wife. By you.

Wife: How?

Meera: I'll tell you in some time. But first you need to tell me what else would you have done other than taking up a job?

Wife: Experience something I never have.

Meera: Like?

Wife: I don't know how to say it.

Meera: Just type it out. Don't think too much.

Wife: I want to experience what it is to 'date' a man. We never dated. We never got to know each other. We were shown photographs of each other. That's all. Even after getting married we hardly got to know each other. When did we ever chat like this?

Meera: So you want to date other men?

Wife: If you were not there. I want to know if every man is the same. If every man thinks of, sees and treats women similarly. Do I feel different in different men's company or is it the same? I read a book that discussed the concept of soulmates. Is it necessary to be someone's domestic partner to qualify as his or her soulmate?

Meera: I won't be clichéd and say all men are same. Maybe it depends on luck.

Wife: I don't think I have ever felt lucky.

There is a thoughtful pause. Both women know they are online but neither is typing.

Meera: Do I satisfy you sexually? Be honest. I won't judge you. Or be angry.

There is another long pause; the wife is online.

* * *

5 a.m.

Meera notices that the wife is typing, erasing, then typing again. This happens a few times. It makes her restless.

Meera: What is it?

The response time is shorter than Meera's anticipation.

Wife: Why is it that if a wife shows her sexual prowess on bed she too is labelled a whore?

Meera: Have I done that?

Wife: Many a time. I don't blame you if you don't remember since you were drunk. I don't remember if we ever were intimate when you were sober. Even on our first night together you were drunk.

Meera: Let me tell you, there's no woman in this world who hasn't been labelled a whore, either verbally or in a man's mind. To treat women as filth is arousing for many men. Exceptions are always there but I'm afraid the generalization holds true.

Wife: Does that mean you have never respected me?

Meera: Think. Think hard. Then answer: what do you feel?

Wife: No.

Meera: Now answer my previous question. Do I satisfy you sexually?

Wife: No.

Meera: Have I ever?

Wife: No.

Meera: I don't satisfy you sexually. I don't respect you, and still you seek my validation, put me on a pedestal simply because I'm your husband?

Wife: What other option do I have?

Meera: Meera too didn't have an option. If she had said the same thing to herself she would have been sold to that sheikh in Dubai. But you know what, it was only when she had no other option that she decided to run away, and she has never looked back on that decision. She is happy doing what she is because at the end of the day she is in a position to bring a smile on her daughter's face. And this made her hopeful that a little bit of tomorrow is perhaps under her control.

Wife: But I can't do that. Meera had to run away because she was going to be sold. If I do that, I will be a bad woman because you are my husband. You have given me a house, children; because of you I get food. If I run away, all fingers will point at me. Everyone's. Even yours. I don't know if Meera knows this but being a whore is still easier than being a wife.

Meera: Just like Meera isn't a whore *only*, you aren't a wife *only*. These labels act as blinders. They deter us from seeing ourselves as we truly are. A woman is defined by the roles society ascribes to her. If a woman is successful at work and not at home, she isn't excused. But if a man is even moderately successful at work, then it is assumed that his wife is lucky to have him. Cutting a long debate short, the more you care about those fingers, give a damn about them, the more will they seem in number. Think about yourself. Think about your kids. Do you want your daughters to study only till class X? To be married only to lose their virginity to a drunk husband? To be ill-treated in front her husband's friends? To remain sexually dissatisfied and unaware of the pleasures that their own bodies can achieve?

Wife: I'm confused. Is my husband asking me to rebel against him?

Meera: Yes, I am. And now if you say Meera has fucked up my mind then it has probably happened for the better, I believe.

Wife: What exactly should I do?

Meera: The moment I'm home I want you to slap me first.

Wife: What are you saying?

Meera: Yes. You heard me, promise me that you'll slap me.

Wife: How can I?

Meera: Tell me haven't I slapped you yet?

Wife: Yes, you have. Many times.

Meera: Then you have to just do that to me when I'm home next. Don't hit me in front of my kids. Just let me enter the bedroom. Then slap me hard. If I pretend to not be aware of this chat, then show your phone to me. And tell me on my face that you know everything about my whores. And if I don't mend my ways, you will show the chat to everyone.

Wife: My hands are shaking. Isn't this some kind of . . . blackmail?

Meera: This is what one needs to do when the rights one deserves aren't given to one.

Wife: Are you sure of what you are asking me to do?

Meera: I'm not asking. This is what you are doing when we are in the bedroom after I come back from this tour.

Wife: I don't know what to say. Okay, I promise.

Meera: Good. That's like my wife.

Wife: Really?

Meera: Yes. Trust me, the harder you slap, the stronger will your hold be on our relationship.

Wife: If I get to steer our relationship, I won't let it hit any obstacle.

Meera: I know that. But you also have to promise me that you will pursue a graduation course. Even if it's through correspondence. You should still do something other than parenting. It is important to be independent.

Wife: I feel so liberated suddenly. To be honest, I have never awaited your homecoming more eagerly. I'm happy I texted you tonight.

Meera: Yes. Good that you texted.

Wife: I have texted you earlier as well, during your other trips but you never responded. But today . . .

Meera: It's all because of that Meera.

Wife: I think I like her.

Meera: I think I like her too. Don't worry, not more than you.

Wife: Hahaha! Thanks to our chatting, I didn't even realize it's almost morning now.

Meera: Yes, it's *almost morning*. Do make it count. Bye now.

Wife: See you soon.

* * *

6 a.m.

There is a beep. But it is her pimp. He wants to know if she is done. Meera responds: 'Almost. Will be down in five minutes.'

She glances at her client. He is still snoring. Meera deletes the messages exchanged with his wife in the past couple of hours and places the phone right where it was. She walks towards the huge window in the room. Her eyelids are heavy with sleep. But she still manages to smile at the view outside. She has never smiled after a night with a client. Everything is still outside. No chaos. Meera has a sudden urge to know what his wife looks like. She goes back to his phone and opens the photo gallery. The first few pictures are of her and a few other women—the pimp must have sent him for selection. She swipes one picture after another. After a series of pornographic photos, she finally comes across a photo of three children. One is around twelve years old, the other no more than five or six and the youngest doesn't seem to be more than two. An ironical smile spreads on her face. All of them are girls. She hopes her client will one day understand how to respect women; he is the father of three after all. She swipes left. The next picture is that of her client and a woman wearing a heavy sari, her face half covered by the *ghunghat*. Meera magnifies the picture but the face isn't visible. Only the outline of her nose and chin is there, which is enough for her to guess that she is beautiful. She is a bit on the heavy side but that's not her problem, not a permanent one at least. Meera sighs. Her real problem is snoring away on the bed in the hotel. Meera hopes the wife welcomes him the way she has promised her. Deep within she knows that what she sensed in the wife are mere embers, but if fanned correctly, they can still burn the solid patriarchal house down. She doesn't know if the wife will actually slap her husband. What will happen after that? Will she show some spirit and move out with the kids till the husband redeemed himself? She will never know. But she will always know that she convinced a woman to slap her own husband because it had been long overdue. A smile lights up her face.

Her phone beeps. Her train of thought pauses. She checks the message. It's the pimp again.

'How much longer? Any problem?'

'No, no. Coming down,' she replies.

Meera wastes no time in taking off her bathrobe, wearing her dress and leaving.. This isn't the first time that she is leaving a five-star hotel at dawn. But for the first time, she is leaving one feeling a dawn within her as well.

Weekends

First Weekend

It has been three years since Kratika and Devang got married. A dreamy romance on social media; a dreamier wedding in their hometown, Bhopal. They stay and work at Bengaluru. Kratika (twenty-eight) works for an international tours and travel company as a customer relationship officer while Devang (thirty) works as a team lead in a call centre. They are good with their savings; their future is planned. They want to first buy a 2BHK flat and then plan for a child. That is why Devang didn't stop Kratika from working a year and a half after their wedding. Kratika used to work before getting married. The first year was their honeymoon period. From the second year onwards, Devang realized that it was important for one partner to earn and the other to save. So Kratika took up a job again. But neither knew that work would keep them from seeing each other all week. Their timings didn't match. Kratika would leave at nine in the morning and come back around eight. Devang would leave at five in the evening and come home around six in the morning. When he was at home, she was still asleep. When she came back, there was no one at home. The couple only had the weekend to spend with each other. But there too was a dilemma. Should they have lunch or dinner outside, party with their friends lest they were labelled social outcasts, or go shopping, finish pending household chores, or have sex? And if everything fell into place, someone from Bhopal was always visiting them for at least a week, or for two weekends, to be more specific.

After stalling sex for a long time, the couple finally found a weekend to spend solely with each other and no distractions around. Kratika bought vanilla candles and some sexy lingerie, and even got a bikini wax done. Sex was always about the ambience for her. Devang, on the other hand, had a collection of her favourite flavoured condoms and also brought her favourite male perfume online. They were ready for the night. But an hour into the foreplay, Devang couldn't get it up.

'What's happening?' a worried Kratika asked.

'I don't know. It was all right yesterday evening,' a panicked Devang said, looking at his limp penis. Never before did he have to wait for an erection for this long. Kratika used her hands, her mouth and whatever tricks she knew but to no avail. Frustrated, she gave up. Devang didn't know what to say or do. They had been waiting for this night for a long time. He was busy staring at his penis, as if a good look could make it stand up, when Kratika asked, 'May I ask you something?'

She has never used that phrase before, Devang thought. He nodded.

'Are you bored of me?'

'Are you mad? No!'

'This has never happened before,' she said, pointing towards his flaccid penis.

'Of course, it hasn't.'

'In fact, there were times when you would get a boner just looking at me.'

It sounded like an accusation, which was followed by an awkward silence. Devang looked at her furtively. While he was hoping for some magic, Kratika was wondering if they had enough tricks left for any magic. The realization was so sudden that she went blank. What if it was true: Devang had actually become bored of her?

'You said it was working fine yesterday evening,' she said. Devang had instantly regretted after saying it earlier but was hoping she wouldn't catch it. But he forgot she was his wife. He had heard from his friends, on a lighter note though, that the moment a woman became a wife, god granted her extra sensitivity towards anything her husband said.

'Hmm,' Devang mumbled.

'Were you watching porn?'

'No . . .' Devang said softly, turning over the words in his mind that he was about to say.

'Then?'

'There is this . . . this woman . . . in my office.'

'What's her name?'

'Priyanka.'

'You like her?'

'It's not like I like her but . . .'

'But your penis does.' Kratika was curt.

'Look, it was one of those moments. Meant nothing. Really.'

'I understand,' she said.

'You do?'

'I meant I understand how Priyanka must have felt if she saw you.'

'I don't think she did. But what do you mean?'

'Leave it.'

'No, tell me.'

'Okay, there is this guy in my office. Swastik.'

Devang felt his heart hammering against his ribs.

'I think he lusts for me.'

Kratika never minced her words unlike Devang. He wasn't interested in what another man thought of his wife. At twenty-eight, Kratika was a head-turner. She had a supple, clear skin, lustrous hair, expressive eyes and a naturally curvaceous figure; Devang knew it would only be natural for any man to look at her twice. What he was interested to know was what Kratika thought of Swastik.

'The way your thing starts working after seeing Priyanka, his does after seeing me,' she said. There was a hint of amusement in her voice.

'What about you?'

Kratika turned to stare at Devang and said, 'What about me?'

'Do you like him?' Devang asked, shivering at the thought.

'I have never thought about him. Firstly, he is four years younger to me. All right, he is handsome and well-dressed most of the time. You know how much I adore well-dressed men, right? That's about it.' Kratika moved her hand and casually hit something. She looked down. Devang too followed her sight. He had a raging hard-on. Neither said it but they knew they had found a remedy to make Devang's penis erect and to spice up their boring sex life.

* * *

Second Weekend

When couples are done exploring each other's bodies a little too much, it's time to explore their minds. The mind has something exciting to offer every time. If you are fishing hard for it, that is.

Devang and Kratika understood this when they tried to have sex the previous weekend. And although Kratika hadn't told him much about Swastik, Devang could still feel all the blood rushing down south. Neither had waited for another weekend to arrive so desperately. They told each other they would narrate their fantasies to fish out the requisite arousal for themselves.

'Let me go first,' Devang said.

'All right.'

'Sure.'

They were lying naked on bed. Their phones were switched off and the lights were dimmed. Devang began talking.

Devang's Fantasy

'Priyanka is one of those people whom you suddenly notice one day, even though she may have been working with you for a long time. Let's suppose there is an office party at some pub. Usually Priyanka wears Indian outfits but that night, she wears a little black dress. She looks drop dead gorgeous. Those natural curls of her, the long eyelashes, the innocuous eyes and the dimpled smile. I just realized, I have noticed a lot about her. She is also shy. So I'm the one who goes up to her in the party. She isn't holding any drink. I ask why. She doesn't drink. I'm assuming this because she doesn't look like she drinks. I suggest she should have a breezer at least. She thinks for a few seconds and says okay. I find the way her lips part to gulp down the drink very arousing. The way we have to lean towards each other, shout words into the each other's ears because of the loud music, fills my head with amorous thoughts. I tell her the crowd, the music, the noise is getting to me. If only we could go out and talk. She looks around and nods. I finish my beer; she finishes her breezer quickly. We navigate our way through the crowd at the disc. I am behind her and put an arm around her shoulder to help her walk through the crowd. For once, I place my hand on her waist. She doesn't complain, as if it is a normal gesture. We get out of the pub. There's a chill in the air. I ask her if she is feeling cold. She nods. I suggest we sit inside my car and talk. She agrees. We walk towards the parking lot in silence. With such a steep sexual tension between us, silence is our best foreplay. We sit inside my car. I don't know what to say. She smiles awkwardly and I do the same. I switch on the FM channel. I am about to change the station when she tries to switch on the heater. Our fingers touch accidentally. We look at each other and the next moment Priyanka's lips are on mine. And then . . . and then . . .'

Devang looks at Kratika. She has a smile on her face. It makes him smile too. He has a semi-hard-on by now.

'Girls are so easy in a guy's fantasy, isn't it? She would have slapped you if you had held her by the waist like that,' she sniggers.

Devang laughs out loud. Kratika is right, of course.

'Also, how come you let her lead?'

'I don't know. Maybe since you are beside me, I'm a little wary of what you might say if I'd said I pounced on her.'

'What a gentleman of a husband I have. On the one hand he is telling me his fantasy of another woman and on the other he is behaving as if whatever happened in the fantasy is because of the woman. Wow, I love you, Devang.'

Devang kisses Kratika's cheek in delight.

Kratika's Fantasy

'Swastik is no Mr Desirable. It's not that he isn't good-looking, well dressed but, you know, not my type. This along with the fact that he is younger than me makes it difficult for me to fantasize about him but I will still try. Maybe the only thing that turns me on about him is the way he looks at me. Okay, I imagine it is night-time and the office is almost empty. Only Swastik is there and, of course, me too. We are finishing our work. We sit close to each other, separated by only two chairs. I find him looking at me through a mirror in front of us. He is giving me those prying looks. The moment our eyes lock, he hastily looks down. I know the leverage is with me. Else he would've maintained his gaze. There is something in him that is holding him back from what he has on his mind. As if the moment our eyes meet, I will read his mind and judge him. But I enjoy it this way. It gives me a sense of power. You know how much I like to control these things, Devang, don't you?

'The next time he looks into the mirror, I open my bottle and drink water while looking at him. I finish my water but pretend to be thirsty. Swastik immediately offers me his bottle. I take it, thank him and drink obscenely. The way Priyanka did while drinking her breezer, I imagine. This time Swastik interrupts. He says he has drank from it before. I pause, give a slightly devilish look and tell him it's okay. And gulp down the water, all the while staring at him. My chair has wheels. So I wheel myself over to him and thank him, looking deep into his eyes. He can't take his eyes off of me.

'A minute later I get up. He gets up too. Work's done. It's time to leave. We go to the elevator together. I know he has things to tell me but he doesn't. When a woman makes a man stack up things inside him, he is like a volcano waiting to erupt. I love that thought. The fact that I'm not letting him erupt. We step inside the elevator together. There's no one else. The door closes. We are going down to the ground floor; our office floor is on the seventh. After the fifth floor, the elevator clangs to a stop. There's a power cut. It is pitch dark inside. I don't react. He switches on his phone's torchlight. We can hear each other breathing urgently in the silence. He points the torchlight towards me. Drops of sweat trickle down my forehead. He slowly points the torchlight downwards on my body. As if he is stripping me. It's damn arousing. He takes a step closer. We stare at each other intensely, He tries to come closer but we hear someone trying to open the door from outside. It's one of the security guards. The door is yanked open but we are still a few feet above the ground. Swastik jumps down first. He urges me to jump as well and says that he will catch me. Our bodies rub against each other when he catches me. I feel his hardness as he puts me down on the floor.'

Kratika stops. Few seconds later, Devang says, 'Go on. I'm listening.'

She holds his rock-hard penis and whispers into his eyes, 'I know you have been listening.'

'So, what happens next?' His mouth has gone dry.

'Fantasy ends.'

'You are not going to . . .'

'I'm going to . . . with my husband. In reality.' Kratika smiles at him seductively. Devang swallows nervously as if in a spell.

'See, your wife wasn't easy in her fantasy as well,' Kratika says, chuckling.

'But I dare you to be difficult now,' Devang says and flips her to get on top. By the time they are done, they are gasping for air.

* * *

Third Weekend

Devang and Kratika constantly texted each other throughout the week; they found it really funny to see the persons they had fantasized about in real life. They didn't remember the last time they had been looking forward to a weekend so expectantly. Earlier, they would get so caught up with everything that they would realize that it was weekend only at the last moment. But now, they were still taking time out and counting down to the weekend.

Devang's Fantasy

'You remember I'd gone to a house party at a college friend's posh flat in KR Puram a few months ago? I know I'm being repetitive with parties but I like the scenario. I promise it will be different next time.'

'That's fine. Who is judging anyway?' Kratika says softly.

True, Devang thinks and continues. 'So, I'm at this house party. There are a few girls as well. The doorbell rings. It is one our friends. She says she also got along her roommate because she was feeling bored. Everyone in the group says it's fine. For me it's more than fine. Her roommate is Priyanka. I know it's a silly coincidence. But fantasies are about that, no? I notice a twinkle in her eyes when she spots me. I already have a breezer in my hand for her and a beer for myself. But surprising me, she takes the beer instead. I'm impressed. She tells me I'm impressed because I'm surprised. I agree. We chat, which allows us to have three beers on the trot. The way she laughs at whatever I say makes me realize that she is tipsy. I mean, you know for a fact I don't have that good a sense of humour.'

'Or it could mean that she is really interested in you,' Kratika says. Devang throws her a thanks-for-helping-my-cause glance at her. 'I search my pockets and tell her I have forgotten my cigarettes. She says we can go out to buy them. I readily agree. We excuse ourselves. We go to the elevator but find that it's not working. So we decide to take the stairs. But Priyanka suggests we take the backstairs, saying that the view from there is fantastic. I follow her and realize that it's an open staircase and indeed has a view of the city line. We are on the sixteenth floor. I ask her incredulously if she climbed sixteen floors. She says they took the elevator but her roommate had a smoke here before entering.'

'Unnecessary detail,' Kratika laments.

'Sorry,' Devang says.

'I'm about to climb down the stairs when I hear a giggle. It's Priyanka. She says she is reminded of what her roomie and she were discussing minutes ago standing in the staircase. "What?" She stops smiling and climbs down the stairs to reach me. She stops on the stair above mine, places her hands on my shoulder and tells me to sit down. I do so as if under a spell. She too sits down putting her hand right on my groin and slowly unzips my jeans and puts her hand inside. My jaws drop. I start breathing faster. And when I realize she has my penis inside her mouth, my eyes shut. She gives me the best blowjob of my life. Like the best of the best . . .'

'Sorry, I'm not comparing. Just went with the flow,' Devang sounds apologetic.

'No offence taken, Mr,' Kratika says. 'What happens then?' she asks.

'She makes me come. It's done. You know I come only once in a night.'

'Now, tell me what you have in mind?'

Kratika smiles teasingly.

'Just don't make it a long one,' Devang says, glancing at his erection.

Kratika's Fantasy

'I close my eyes. I see rains. Incessant rains. Then I see myself trying to book an Ola/Uber. Nothing is available. I don't know what to do. I'm standing next to the exit of our office premises. The world outside is murky. The kind that makes you feel today is probably the last day of the world. And it wants to sign off making everyone feel scared, depressed and frustrated. I try to call you but there's some network problem.

'Is it okay if I mention you in my fantasy?' Kratika asks.

'Yeah, sure. But only to the extent you did just now,' Devang says. They don't look at each other. Kratika's eyes are closed.

'I don't know what to do. That's when I hear someone honking. I realize it's Swastik. He gestures me to get inside. I hurriedly get inside the car. We make small talk as he pulls out of the office premises.

'The drive is slow because of the traffic. Swastik wants to focus on me but has to do so with his eyes on the road lest he hits someone or some vehicle. I decide to tease him a bit. I casually turn and spot a tissue box in the rear seat. I lean in such a way that I come close to him. Swastik tells me he loves the way I smell, that he wanted to tell me so the other evening in the elevator but couldn't. We keep talking till I start wiping my cleavage with a tissue. He is deliberately driving slowly as the road ahead is somewhat clear. He is dying to look at me out of the corners of his eyes but is unable to. I find that sexy. I keep the tissue on the dashboard. He looks at it as if he would rather be that than a human. I want to burst out laughing but control myself. I know why he is adjusting his legs the way he is. I make some small talk but he finds it difficult to respond with his attention on me. I know he must me itching to stare at my cleavage, but every time he tries to even have a glance I look at him. We reach our housing society. It's still raining. I guide him to our underground parking lot. I tell him there is an elevator that will take me straight to my floor. I bend forwards to thank him: a final opportunity to have a glimpse of what he had been dying to see. I don't stand there waiting for him to have his fill. I leave immediately. But while I'm pressing the elevator button, I hear a sound. Swastik has got out of his car. He is heading towards me. There's an urgency in his walk. Before I can say anything, his lips are on mine, his hands around my waist and mine around his neck. We smooch passionately. His hand slides down to my butt. The way he tightens his grasp on it lets me know that this is only the tip of his passion. As we continue to smooch, a car alarm goes off. Swastik breaks the smooch, takes me to the garage and pushes me between two cars. I know the security guards are there. The alarms must have brought them here. And yet Swastik doesn't stop. He pulls down my leggings and my panties. I've teased him enough. It is time for some pleasurable punishment.'

But Kratika stops talking and instead starts moaning. Devang is behind her. They were lying sideways. He slowly entered her not able to take his arousal any more. It's the spoon pose. They are trying it for the first time.

* * *

Fourth Weekend

There was an unprecedented restlessness in Devang that Kratika noticed while they were dining at a nearby restaurant. She wanted to but didn't tell him about it then. While walking back home, Devang's pace was more hurried than usual. It was only when they were in bed that Kratika said, 'I'm sorry I wanted to tell you this before but . . .'

'No!' The way Devang's face fell trying to guess what it was, was cute.

'It is. I'm chumming. First day. Already paining a bit.'

Devang sighed. And with it his lust too dwarfed a bit.

'It's okay,' he said. Devang had always been understanding, and rarely did a man prioritize his woman's necessities over his urges.

'It's crazy what we have been up to,' she said.

'I know. If someone got to know, we'd be judged harshly.'

'Nobody has to know. But I get what you mean. Even within the four walls of our home, we are still scared of a societal backlash.'

'Seriously! As a couple we decide what works for us and what doesn't. The objective is to break barriers, some of which inherently exist in a man–woman relationship and some that have been introduced by a patriarchal society.'

After a few seconds of silence, Devang laughed out loud.

'What happened?'

'What if our families in Bhopal got to know what we were up to?'

'One of us will be sent to an asylum while the other will be disowned,' Kratika said laughing.

'That's because we can't live beyond the confines of certain adjectives, I think. Whatever we do needs to be bracketed within one acceptable adjective or another.'

'I've thought about it as well. It's a push-pull effect.'

'As in?'

'The heart pushes us to step out of the moral perimeter that we have drawn for ourselves based on whatever has been fed to us emotionally, morally, socially since birth. The push is because the heart works on our primal instinct. Years of manipulation can subjugate it but not completely tame it. While the mind pulls us back telling us the perimeter is where we belong. The mind is socially trained while the heart is habituated to its primal nature.'

'I like the way you broke it up. Makes sense to me. It makes me also question the rigidity of our sexual nature. I think sexuality is inherently and deeply fluid. Just that there has to be a way forward, progression, nature manipulated us into thinking a man only belongs to a woman sexually. It's the reproduction angle that is the basis for us to think like that. Maybe rightly so. I don't know.'

Kratika looked up at Devang and said, 'Is this what happens when a couple have exhausting sex every weekend? The philosophers in them pay a visit?'

'Who knows!' Devang has a sly smile on his face.

* * *

Fifth Weekend

Kratika is brushing her teeth. Although they are non-vegetarians, Kratika can't kiss after having a meat-based dish. She has to brush and makes Devang brush his teeth as well. He has tried talking her out of it but to no avail. This time Devang gives in without arguing.

Kratika tries not to look at the two love bites on her bosom. One has faded and the other is in the process. Only she knows how many times her colleagues had inquired about it. In the past five years since she had known Devang this was the first-ever love bite whose essence had been intact for more than a week. She caressed it with her left hand.

As Kratika gets inside the blanket beside Devang, he lowers the temperature of the AC further. He is already naked. She undresses herself, throwing her nighty and panty on a bean bag in the bedroom. He is smelling nice. She has turned it into a habit of his. To smell good before having sex. It helps Kratika get in the mood. Only he doesn't know that she's already in the mood since she saw her love bites in the bathroom minutes ago.

'You know . . .' Devang starts but Kratika places her palm over his mouth.

'Tonight, I'll narrate first,' she says. He nods. He doesn't know what she has on her mind.

What if I change the scenario a little bit tonight? What if I make it a little edgy? I've been playing the tease for some time now, but what if I play the submissive one tonight? Kratika wonders.

'To imagine your partner being submissive to someone else takes eroticism to a whole new level,' Devang whispers.

'You remember the night I was out till the wee hours partying?' she asks.

He frowns before saying, 'Yeah, your company was the official travel sponsor for the Indian women's cricket team or something, right?'

'That's right. Let me take you there. Placing a fantasy in between a reality is a different kind of high.'

Devang shifts his legs. Perhaps his loins are on fire already. Kratika closes her eyes.

Kratika's Fantasy

'I'm in Taj Vivanta. I can almost hear the loud music, cheering, tapping footsteps, and clinking of glasses. Most of my colleagues and seniors are quite drunk. I'm on my third drink. And in between all the madness, the party chaos and disco lights, I find Swastik's gaze on me. As if I'm his property that no one else can claim. Till my second drink, I had been playing along furtively. But after gulping down my third drink, I'm staring back at him brazenly. We are digging into each other's flesh through our eyes. I can sense I'm getting somewhat wet between my legs. And just when I want this to go on forever, he leaves the room. I wonder why. I finish my drink. I try to guess why he left. About ten minutes later, I see him again. He doesn't waste time staring and instead directly approaches me. I feel a shiver run down my spine. He whispers into my ears, "I've booked a room here. I walk out. You follow. Room number 301."

'His confidence that I will indeed follow him arouses me. I feel that if I don't follow him now, not only will I disappoint him but also myself. I go to the bar and ask for my fourth drink. When I'm handed the drink, I finish it in one go. I dash out of the hall, into the elevator and in no time find myself outside room number 301. I knock only to realize the door is ajar. I push it open. Only a lamp next to the windows is on; the rest of the room is in darkness. Swastik is sitting on a chair next to the lamp. He tells me he knew I would come. When a man second guesses a woman's will, it can go two ways: either the woman can be supremely scared or she is superlatively aroused. Do I even need to tell you which one I am? I take a few steps but he asks me to stop. Then he utters one word and my skin is immediately dotted by goose pimples. "Strip." I do as I am told. You remember what I had worn that night? A thin strap, white, knee-length dress. So I don't have to work hard. I only pull down the straps and the dress comes undone. I unhook my white bra. Swastik asks me to stop and come over to where he is sitting. I do as I am told. He asks me to kneel down. He places the tip of his tongue on the nape of my neck and licks me till the end of my spine. He clenches my panty with his teeth and tugs it down.'

Kratika hears a grunt and frowns.

'Are you with me, Devang?' Kratika asks. There is no sound. She opens her eyes.

'I'm sorry but I came,' he says apologetically. Kratika looks at him and then below. *Indeed*. She bursts out laughing, looking at his face. Devang has never looked so cute before.

'So no action tonight?' she asks him teasingly.

'Shut up. You and your fantasies just don't spare me,' he says, and scampers towards the bathroom to clean himself.

My supposed fantasy is controlling the reality of my husband, Kratika thinks. She feels like an evil sorceress as she smiles.

* * *

Sixth Weekend

They didn't expect that after an exhausting week they would fight over who was going to narrate a fantasy first. Kratika suggested they toss a coin.

'I don't believe this,' Devang said.

'You have to, else let me narrate first.'

'No way. You get into details and then it becomes difficult for me to even think about anything else.'

Kratika giggled. Devang switched on the lights and went to the wardrobe to get his wallet. Kratika sat up on the bed. He took out a two-rupee coin and was about to flip it when he stopped.

'What happened?' Kratika asked.

'I've an idea. Can't we role play instead of fantasizing?'

'What exactly do you have in mind?' Kratika seemed intrigued.

'I can play Swastik for you.'

'And you want me to play Priyanka?'

'We'll see. First your scenario.'

'This is different. Interesting. So, the scenario is . . .'

'No. The other person gives you the scenario.'

'Why is my husband sounding so erotic tonight?' Kratika looked amused.

'Don't tell me you aren't happy about it.' Devang came back to bed.

'I am. So what's the scenario?'

'I'm Swastik. I follow you from office because I'm obviously smitten by you. But I don't follow you till your housing society. I come up to your house and ring the doorbell.'

'I've a feeling this will be the sexiest,' Kratika said lying down.

Devang got inside the blanket, lowered the AC to a minimum and took off his clothes. Kratika undressed as well.

'I press the doorbell. Ding dong.'

'Come on! That sound was so unnecessary,' Kratika said.

'Okay. I press the doorbell,' Devang said. His eyes were open while Kratika's were closed.

'I think it's you and open the door rather quickly but casually too.'

'Do you do that? Open the door casually when you know it's me?'

'Are you going to break from time to time and ask questions?'

'I'm sorry.'

'I open the door but I'm a little surprised to see Swastik.'

'Surprised or shocked?'

'Surprised.'

'Which means you're happy to see him?'

'Yes. In the fantasy.'

'Right. So, I, Swastik, greet you first and then tell you I was in the same building visiting a friend when I saw you entering it. Thought I'd say hi.'

'That's a good thing you did. I was going to make some tea for myself, and some company to go along with it will be great.'

'Thank you for welcoming me. I step inside. Look around. What are you wearing by the way?'

'I'm in my shorts and a spaghetti top.'

'Won't you feel uncomfortable wearing that in front of an office colleague who has come to your place unannounced?'

'What is it with you and questions tonight?'

Devang couldn't tell Kratika that although he had enjoyed the weekend sessions, he had felt jealous that she could actually be submissive to her colleague in her mind. He knew it was a fantasy but he couldn't keep the hotel striptease out of his mind throughout the week. The role play wasn't just a random idea. He wanted to see how far she'd go.

'Answer me.'

'Yes. In my fantasy I will be all right with it.'

'But we are our real selves in our fantasies.'

'What do you mean?'

'Nothing. Let's carry on. I check out your figure when you go inside the kitchen. I follow you inside on the pretext of checking out the flat.'

'I tell you my husband isn't at home.'

'Do you say that as a matter of fact or are you hinting at an opportunity?'

'As an opportunity, of course.'

'Hmm. I come close to you while you're putting the pan on the *chulha* and hold your waist from behind.'

'I close my eyes and moan slightly.'

'Does that mean you were waiting for it?'

'I thought you liked me being submissive.'

'Submissive is different. Playing easy is different.'

'You are killing the mood tonight.' Kratika opened her eyes and looked at her husband.

'I want to know if you really like Swastik or is it only in your fantasies?'

'Where is this coming from? Did I ask you if you really lust for Priyanka?'

'What if I really lust for her? All right, I do. Now you answer.'

Kratika glared at him. Soon her eyes flooded with tears. She put on her clothes and ran into the bathroom. For some time, Devang sat still. He was brooding. Then he heard her sobbing. He started regretting what he had told her. He got out of the bed, wore his underwear and knocked on the bathroom door.

'Kratika?' He knocked. 'Look, I'm sorry. Will you please open the door? Please? We can stop this stupid role play and get back to narrating fantasies. I swear I won't ask any more questions.'

Devang sat outside the bathroom while Kratika stayed inside. Neither of them slept.

* * *

Seventh Weekend

Last week was different. They only talked through messages and even those were few and far in between. Just the basic:

Did you eat?

Did you reach home?

I'll be late.

Please pay the electricity bill.

Maid will come a little late today. Don't keep sleeping. Do open the door.

On Friday Kratika informed Devang that her relatives from Bhopal were in Bengaluru. If she didn't pay them a visit at the hotel where they were staying, they might end up coming to their house. Devang asked Kratika to handle it as he had work. He will be home the next morning, Saturday. They wanted to forget what had happened last weekend but didn't know how.

Devang's Reality

The work load is an excuse. I'm with Priyank. There is no Priyanka. The addition and deletion of one letter from my lover's name makes my truth a lie and my lie a truth. The fact that I no longer feel sexually aroused by Kratika is because I like Priyank. I'm unapologetic about it when it comes to my conscience. So what if I'm gay (or maybe bisexual)? I think it is none of anyone's business what my sexual orientation is. But when it comes to declaring this to Kratika, I run out of confidence. I don't want to lose her. I love her so much that when she mentions another man, I still feel jealous. When she narrated the hotel fantasy to me, I was consumed with rage for a whole week. It disturbed me even though I knew it was only a part of her fantasy. Even though I know I have dirtier secrets. I didn't want to subject her to any interrogation but somehow the situation deteriorated and it ended up being one. I really love her.

But I love Priyank as well. Only I know that the fantasies I've narrated to Kratika in the past few weeks were based

143

on real events. The first time I had connected with Priyank was indeed during an office party, following which we had made out. Kratika thinks I get erect thinking about her fantasies, but the truth is I feel the rush of blood thinking about Priyank. And it is not just a sexual relationship. We are emotionally invested as well. How do I explain it to her without her wanting to leave me? Just because a husband and wife stop connecting sexually, doesn't mean that their relationship is over.

I see Priyank getting our frappes from the counter. We are at Starbucks. We plan to spend the night together. Unlike Kratika, I don't have to share any fantasies with Priyank. But tonight's details may become my next weekend's fantasy. I hope she forgives me and the game continues.

Kratika's Reality

No relative is visiting Bengaluru this week. Swastik is running a temperature. He has nobody but me in the city. I've been having an affair with him for the past eight months now. I know how it started. Funnily, even Devang, by now, knows how it started. I still remember that night when Swastik and I were alone in office. The power cut in the elevator. And the rest of the story as well. Even the party in the hotel. Although I pretended to be pricey in my fantasies, the truth is I was pretty easy for Swastik. If someone asked who he was to me, I would say, my stress buster. This entire affair has been that for me. It definitely doesn't mean I don't love Devang. I will never leave him. Honestly, I never thought I would be able to confess everything to him. Though I meant it as a confession, he heard it as a fantasy. I feel lighter, better. Last weekend I wasn't hurt but his interrogation made me feel guilty.

There is a sexual tension between Swastik and me, but we have rarely had penetrative sex. He has been in a long-distance marriage. And what he and I are doing is filling up the need for belonging. I stay with Swastik in office more than I stay with Devang at home. One of those perils of a modern-day lifestyle, I guess. There have been times when I desperately craved for both of them to be one person, knowing fully well the impossibility of it.

In the last three years, I have realized that after a relationship reaches the destination of a domestic partnership, the persons involved stop seeking love in each other. What we seek, rather, is a comfort zone—a zone that isn't allowed to us anywhere else and with nobody else. As long as the affair with Swastik doesn't push me out of the comfort zone I seek with Devang, I won't feel guilty. But if it does . . . well, as of now, I'm waiting for tomorrow night. I know Devang. The short messages tell me he will apologize tomorrow. And I will happily dress my reality as a fantasy and present it in front of my husband. We shall make love like there is no tomorrow on yet another weekend.

The Flight Is on Time

From: Siya Mishra
Reply to: Siya*****@*****.com
To: rammohanmishra**@*****.com
Date: Saturday, 7 July 2007, 7.07 a.m.
Subject: Hello
Mailed by: *****.com
Signed by: *****.com

Hi Ram,

This is Siya, your wife. This is no virus attack. I know I have never mailed you before; I didn't have an email id till a few minutes ago. I have created one because there are things I need to tell you. When a wife has to resort to emailing in order to communicate with her husband, one realizes how frivolous, damaged and brittle their relationship has become. I could have told you whatever I'm going to write here face-to-face, but I chose not to. *Choice* . . . can you even imagine how empowered I feel already?

I wanted to put down all my thoughts, opinions, observations and complaints about us so you can come back to these words again and again. I want these words to burn a hole first into your mind and then into your soul. I want you to be tormented by my words the same as I have by yours. No matter how much I try to shut them out, I can't.

I want you to read this email again and again to feel the pain that I have felt. I know you will. For you won't have anything else to fall back on except this email once you finish reading it. Maybe you won't read it again for months due to anger as your ego will be hurt. Once that subsides, you'll read this email again. And again and again.

Every time you read this email, you will realize what a failure of a husband you have been.

Ram, I'm pregnant.

The obvious question is: whose baby is it? Between you and me, we know the answer. But even if you have a niggling doubt, let me put it to rest: it's not *ours*. Do you remember last December you had told me about some colleague whose wife was having an extramarital affair? And in a fit of suspicion demanded to know if I too had a lover as you weren't around for most of the year. I'm sure you didn't care how much that question hurt me. That one question immediately erased my years of devotion to and love for you. What did I do to deserve it? Did I give you cause for concern? You sounded pretty certain that I had been going behind your back. But then that incident made me introspect. And introspection sometimes helps rekindle a latent courage in oneself. Courage to tell oneself that whatever happened to date is fine but nothing like this should ever happen again.

I had been taught since childhood that a woman can't love herself. A woman's love is mostly about sacrifice, and the rest about acceptance. And if there is something left, it's about adjustment. Many a time in order to hold on to that love, which is also the basis of our identity in the society that we live in, we let go of our individuality. We have to live the way our fathers and husbands want us to, and later as the society wants us to. We are seldom who we really are. We have no choice but to withdraw and lead interiorized lives, fighting to keep our real selves alive in our minds. That's all that we have. And that accusation of yours challenged the real me, woke her up. Men always find a higher ground to stand on whereas women have to stand on their toes, struggling to reach that height. The ones who manage to do it are given dirty labels. Why?

One afternoon, like any other afternoon, when I had nothing better to do, I had secretly compared our mark sheets, from high school to higher secondary to graduation. And you know what? I had always scored more than you. I was more studious; I could have earned as well as you. Maybe more. But my father didn't let me study after graduation, let alone work. Who would marry a woman who earns for herself? A wife can't be a husband's competition. A husband should be, however, a wife's master. Maybe your parents and friends think you are an ideal son and friend, but not me. You ceased to be a good husband that night in December when you uttered those words. You didn't make the cut for me, Ram, and you won't ever.

It has been exactly 1507 days since we got married. Can you remember a single day when I did not carry out my responsibilities as a wife? Every day, on weekends, holidays and weekdays alike, I would get up at 6.30 a.m. Never a minute more or less. I didn't even use an alarm clock for the past few years whereas as a child I could never wake up early. I changed my biological clock for you. *For you*! The least that you could have done was be a little grateful about it. I would get up, take a bath, worship, and by seven was in the kitchen preparing breakfast for you and your parents. Then I would prepare lunch, take care of your father, massage his rheumatic leg for half an hour. Did I ever ask you to get a maid to do the work for papa? I would then cook a pure vegetarian meal for your religious mother and a different one for us. Fine, I told myself. With the exhaust fan not working every other day, do you realize how difficult it must have been for me to stay cooped up in the kitchen all the time? It was like a furnace during the summers. I wiped the sweat off my brows a thousand times for you! But to you, all this was insignificant. Why?

Just because you've been brought up to take your wife for granted? Yes, it is my duty to keep you happy, to go an extra mile for you. But tell me, isn't it also a husband's duty to keep his wife satisfied, in life, in bed?

I remember our first night. I was shy and so were you. And when we stripped, I was expecting an earth-shattering orgasm. But you couldn't give me one, not on our wedding night or on our honeymoon or ever! Every time you came inside me, you looked flushed with satisfaction. I *faked* having a good time for you! Did you ever try to find out if I was satisfied? No. You assumed that I was satisfied because you were satisfied. If I would have discussed it with you, you would've thought that I was complaining; that my sexual appetite was not normal; that I was horny. And a horny woman is never respected anywhere. I would have been at a loss even if I had not satisfied you, or shown an interest in you. You'd have rejected me immediately. The point here is not whether you satisfied me or not. It is whether you at all cared for my satisfaction? Did you, even for a second, think that I too deserved satisfaction? My emotions were always invisible to you. Honestly, if you had felt them, cared for them, I wouldn't have been required to write this email.

There were nights when I'd want to have sex but you weren't interested. I did pester you for a while in the beginning because I assumed that if you could have me when I wasn't in the mood then I too could have you when you weren't that keen. Isn't marriage about taking care of the spouse's needs? Or at least respecting them? But when you told me that being horny doesn't suit a wife, I understood that I hadn't married the man I had thought I had. I had an idea of my perfect guy. Of course, I never expected anyone to live up to those expectations, but, Ram, you fell short majorly. After that demeaning comment of yours, I was both happy and sad. Happy because I thought I too could say no to you when I wasn't in the mood and sad because you were fine not ever asking about it.

I never made a fuss again. But on nights when you were horny and I wasn't interested (because I was exhausted after doing all the household chores) you would force yourself, claiming that it's because of women like me that men turn to whores. And such women are even bigger whores. I remember your words clearly; nobody had used such a derogatory term for me earlier. I had never been called a whore before. And it was not a roadside ruffian who had first called me a whore, not lecherous men who gaped at my breasts in markets or rubbed their groins against me in crowded trains, but my husband!

You raped me and I didn't say anything. Did you realize what you had done? If only you had understood my tears and read my silence, my disinterest. If only you had not forced yourself even on days when I was having my periods. Most men are emotionally illiterate. They don't care about their wives, with whom they share a house, a bed, a life, let alone understand women in general. Such emotional abuse made me question my sense of self: maybe I was insignificant. Perhaps I didn't deserve any attention. Maybe there was nothing noticeable in me. Today I know that's the worst thing any man can lead a woman to believe. That she is shit. That's how men control their wives. By gaslighting and drawing lines to circumscribe their movements, actions and desires.

Remember when you had told me that one of your friends had had anal sex and that you wanted to try it as well? I was totally against it but you kept insisting and eventually I relented. I cried and screamed throughout the act; later you left me to my own devices after you were done. It hurt me like crazy for a good three days. I wasn't even able to walk properly but that still wasn't as painful as your insensitivity towards me. If I had told you that I would have liked to tie my husband up and slap him for a sexual high, would you have let me do it?

What do I get in return for years of meekness? An accusation. Was I having an affair behind your back? Maybe you wanted me to have an extramarital affair. Why else would you coax me into wearing those backless blouses every time you took me to your office parties? You always wanted to present me as a prized catch but never treated me as one. Why would you try to convince me to drink alcohol when you knew I didn't like it? Everybody else's wives were drinking so I might as well. You have subjected me to such humiliation. Standing amid your colleagues and their wives, it dawned on me that I was perhaps some decorative object for you.

For the world you were a liberated man, who didn't mind if his wife showed off some skin, but I knew your reality. You just wanted your colleagues to ogle at me and wonder how lucky *you* were. The thought of being every man's envy possibly gave you a kick. You think I didn't understand all this? In spite of being aware of it, I still didn't complain. Why? Have you ever thought of that? It's the same reason why I faked my orgasms with you. To keep your self-respect intact. What if I had told you on your face that you didn't satisfy me sexually and later to my friends? The man who flaunted his score with women didn't really *score* with his wife. And then you had the temerity to ask me if I was having an affair?

We had an arranged marriage. But I used to like a boy before I got married. He was a primary schoolteacher. He liked me too. Although we seldom talked, the exchange of glances was revealing enough. We rarely met. Scandals and slander fly thick and fast in small towns, especially when an unmarried girl is involved. Whenever we met, I wrapped a scarf around my face to avoid being recognized. I didn't like it but we had no other option. One day I told my father I wanted to marry him after my uncle visited us with your proposal. My father argued that a schoolteacher wouldn't be able to keep me happy. But you would. I could have any luxury I wanted if I married you. What my father didn't know was when a woman truly loved a man she could make a comfortable home out of the most basic amenities. I told him I would be happy with the schoolteacher, but he was adamant. He didn't understand. I don't blame him for he too is a man. I never forgot the schoolteacher but slowly accepted my fate.

I can't be your shadow any more, Ram. I have other identities as well. I'm not just your wife. I'm tired of the society dictating my life to me. When was the last time we went out and had something of my choice? We would only go to movies starring your favourite heroines. The restaurant we went to after that was your favourite one. We had even had food that you liked. A third person reading this email might take me for a disgruntled, complaining housewife, but he will never know the pain of remaining invisible to your loved one. But when you had a doubt, I was suddenly all too visible. I suddenly became someone who could have an extramarital affair. We take a bath daily to rinse ourselves of dirt. Tell me, Ram, what kind of spiritual bath do I need to take in order to rinse away this allegation of yours? No, your apology won't work any more. Nor will your pleading and begging. Don't waste your time.

As I mentioned earlier, Ram, I'm pregnant. Who is the father? You'll never know. But I'll give you some clues. If I tell you directly who it is, you won't read this email again and again. He is someone you know very well and yet you will never be able to guess who he is. No matter how much you rack your brains you'll never figure out the answer. And yet if you ever found out, you'd realize that it was so obvious. No, I didn't have an affair with him. I only conceived a child with him. We only did it once. That was good enough. How do you feel, Ram, knowing all this? Yes, now you know how I felt when you asked me that unnecessary and deeply disturbing question last December.

When Madhu, my friend, told me she'd separated from her husband since they were done with each other, I, to be honest, didn't understand her. She too had an arranged marriage. But they lived in the United States and Madhu was independent unlike me. And her husband was truly liberal, unlike you. I couldn't figure out the reason behind their separation. Madhu told me they had decided to stop living with each other and continue being friends. Not that either of them had fallen for anybody else. They just wanted to live separately and see if there was any place for the other in their lives or if it was all an illusion. It was an experiment of sorts. They stayed away from each other for two years and then realized that they should get back together. They are now living happily. This made me wonder if I could do that to us. Leave in order to understand the worth of living together. Sometimes we take each other too much for granted. I wish I could explain this to you. Maybe my absence will. Maybe. But then, even if it does,

I'm not coming back. The father of the child isn't with me. I didn't want his support. If I can carry a child in my womb, I can protect it, shelter it and parent it myself. You probably want to know why I wanted to have a child. Why didn't I stay alone? But understand this that the child is a symbol of all that I had expected from you. Everything that you didn't give me. Whatever we missed as a couple. What we shall never have as a couple. Everything that has forever lost between us. That question was the last nail on the coffin. And believe me, the coffin had been ready from a long time. You got the wood and the nails. I only drilled them in. One day at a time.

I've left the divorce paper, duly signed, under your pillow on the bed. Sign it if you want to, tear it if you want to, or do whatever it is that you want to. Nothing will affect me any more. I am not going to get married again. And I know you won't be able to live without marrying again. Men like you need women for your survival. And then you tell the world that you are self-sufficient. I pity you. Your male ego will probably reject any realization that you might have from this email. It might lead you to call me names. You will add your biased perspective and call it a bitch's story. But guess what, Ram? I. Don't. Give. A. Fuck. Any more.

Your once-upon-a-time wife,
Siya.

157

She presses 'send'.

Siya switches off her phone and fastens her seat belt, staring out of the window. She isn't pregnant. She was bluffing. Her husband deserved it for disrespecting their marriage, making hollow allegations and convincing her that she was worth nothing. It was time to break away from the shackle that her marriage had turned out to be. And in return she shackled her husband, with shame. Ram would live his life believing he wasn't good enough. Once he underwent the pain that she had endured all those years, maybe he'd be redeemed. Who knows? Or he might learn nothing from her desertion of him. If he still continued to believe that she was or capable of having an affair then he would even fail as a human being.

Siya closes her slightly moist eyes and feels relaxed. After long time she is at peace with herself. By giving her husband a chance to further sling mud at her, put her on the societal pyre where everyone would judge her, she feels that she has at last freed herself.

The flight takes off and she feels good that *it is on time*.

Children

Chapter One

They had seen each other before. They remembered. He used to come to the small park in their block in Salt Lake, Kolkata, with his only child. She too used to come there with her only child. Their children attended a small karate class in the park. They had only ever exchanged smiles. Never words. It was only today that they learnt that their sons were in the same school, in the same class. Today they were attending a gathering organized by the school to mourn the death of the thirty-five students and five teachers who had died in an accident during a school excursion. The group was en route to Digha for a two-day excursion. On the bus were also Priyanjali's son and Shayan's. They were both six years old.

They saw each other in the school auditorium, where the gathering had been organized. No words were exchanged. But this time there were no smiles either. They were with their respective spouses. Every parent who had lost their child in the accident was asked to come on stage and light a candle. Prayers were said for the deceased and then the congregation broke up.

For the first two days Priyanjali couldn't even tell herself that whatever had happened had happened for real. The people around her, including her husband, seemed representative of the incident. On the third day she woke up early, prepared her son's tiffin and went to wake him up. She broke down after realizing that he wasn't there, will never be there. Her husband took her to a doctor after she fainted. She was sedated as she had started hallucinating about her son. She was not allowed to attend his funeral lest she had a breakdown.

Five weeks after the incident, the school organized the gathering. By then Priyanjali had slowly started accepting whatever had happened. But she still plodded through life with great difficulty. Her husband tried to be positive, but it only irritated her. *Why did he have to behave as if nothing had happened? As if he had moved on when he clearly hadn't?* She started avoiding him without making it obvious. She no longer dined with him; didn't wait for him to come to bed. She stayed busy in the mornings with the maid, the household chores and left before him, claiming that her office timings had changed. But all she did till it was really time for her to go to office was sit below a Banyan tree opposite to her son's school and watch everyone and no one in particular enter and exit the premises. The hectic routine that she had been used to for the past six years had suddenly been called off. It was as if her limbs had been amputated and she was trying to figure out if her other parts could function the way her hands and feet had. She couldn't adjust to her new routine: of doing nothing except being at home and in office. She always made sure to stop at the park for an evening walk at exactly the time when she took her son to the karate class. The park was the same. The kids practising karate were the same. But the feeling that the sight triggered in her was different.

On one such day when Priyanjali had made herself comfortable on a bench in the park, she realized that someone else was also sitting at the other end. It was the man who used to bring his son to the karate class. He had also lost his son like her.

Shayan had had a nightmare a week before the bus accident. He would break into a cold sweat every time he thought about it. When his son had approached him with the teacher's note seeking permission for the excursion, he had been dead against it. But his wife thought he was being too protective. She convinced him into letting their son go. And now when he was no more, she had packed her bags and left for her parents' house. She had shut herself completely from Shayan, knowing that she wouldn't be able to meet his eyes again. Guilt is a strange emotion. It creates an emotional quicksand that swallows you in bit by bit.

Shayan stayed alone in his huge ancestral house in Salt Lake, with emptiness around and hollowness within. He had been a single child himself; his parents had died a few years ago. But their deaths hadn't been sudden. His father had died of throat cancer and his mother of dengue. In both the cases, he had been ready. But the sudden death of his son haunted him like a vengeful spirit. He wanted to talk to someone. He had always found talking cathartic. He found containing emotions within himself suffocating. But that had become his way of life for the past few weeks. Many a time he felt as if he was having a nightmare, that it would be a matter of minutes before he was woken up by his wife or son. Maybe his wife was a tad too fastidious for his liking but he still loved her. His last words to her before they had sent their son on the excursion were: I told you not to send him. He regrets telling her that. Those words perhaps tightened the noose of guilt that had already wound itself around her after their son's death. He didn't want to but ended up blaming his wife for his death. As if she had sent him knowingly.

After the congregation he went to stay with a friend. Then he shifted to a cheap guest house in the area. He couldn't go back to the house; the empty corridors haunted him. He wouldn't have come to the park either.

Although Shayan was quite expressive, he was also non-confrontational. Perhaps that's why he needed his wife now more than ever. It was while crossing the road to get to the guest house that he noticed the woman that he would see when he would take his son to the karate class enter the park. He had no reason to but decided to head towards the park as well. He sat on a bench watching her take a walk around the park, stop next to the karate class and then walk towards him. She sat on the same bench. She looked lost and withdrawn. The natural glow that she always had seemed dulled. He was in two minds about whether to initiate a conversation or not. He was aching to. For the first time in his life he was desperate to have a listener.

'Shayan Ray,' he said when he caught her eye.

'Priyanjali Chatterjee,' she said softly.

'I know,' he said.

He only said those words: *I know.* She didn't know why but Priyanjali thought he understood as well.

Chapter Two

Priyanjali had left quite abruptly. She didn't even bid Shayan goodbye. He kept sitting on the bench till hunger compelled him to leave the park.

The only thing Priyanjali was looking forward to the next day was a visit to the park in the evening. She had felt as if time had stopped when she was sitting there yesterday. She went to the park in the evening and sat on the same bench. Her eyes were not fixed at anything in particular; her mind brought back memories of the day she had given birth to her son, the labour, the pain. She had opted for a natural birth against the doctor's advice to get a caesarean done. She will never be able to describe how she felt when she saw her child for the first time. Certain emotions are indescribable. They can only be felt, embellished with tears and smiles, but never shared through words. Motherhood, for her, was one such emotion. The memories brought a faint smile on her face, which she was unaware of.

'They were friends.'

Priyanjali heard a man say. She glanced to her right and noticed Shayan sitting at the other end of the bench. When did he come? She hadn't noticed.

'Who? Our kids?' she asked. Shayan nodded.

'I didn't know. What was your son's name?'

'His *daak naam* (nickname) was Titu; Shagnik on the dotted line. Your son was Ashish, right?'

'I called him Binny,' she said, averting her gaze.

'He loved video games. I was supposed to gift him a new one on his birthday,' Shayan said.

'He loved Maggi noodles. Every day he demanded the same for tiffin,' Priyanjali said. They were talking but not looking at each other.

'They used to share it. Titu told me he too loved the way you prepared it.'

Priyanjali looked at Shayan incredulously. Her face slowly broke into a smile.

'I can't believe that Binny shared his Maggi noodles with someone!'

Shayan smiled and said, 'Yes, they were good friends, it seems. Sharing your favourite noodles isn't easy.'

Priyanjali wanted to laugh but checked herself. The smile remained a smile. This time she really looked at him and took in his face. It stayed with her.

'They lived a stop away from each other. Titu would want to walk till Ashish's stop almost every other morning.'

'You could have listened to him once,' she said and immediately realized that the line had been slightly loaded. It might convey a different meaning.

'I mean you didn't listen to your son much?' Priyanjali asked.

'I did, but there were a few occasions when I didn't. For example, I had supported him when he had expressed his ambition to become a soccer player one day.'

'Binny didn't have any ambitions as such. He lived in the present. Of course, he did so unknowingly, but there was no room for the future in his life. It inspired me because I am someone who is always caught in the past and constantly worry about the future.'

'We rarely realize this but sometimes our children are our sorted versions. Even I saw it in Titu.'

'What did you see in him that you had wanted to correct in yourself?'

'I can't take a stand to save my life. And Titu took a stand for our neighbour's son while playing together. I was blown away.'

'How is your wife taking it?' she asked. Shayan didn't respond immediately.

'I'm sorry. Please don't answer if it's personal.'

'It is a personal injury, of course. But not between two people who have the same injury.'

They looked at each other momentarily. It brought them closer than it ought to have.

'My wife is with her parents. She has shut herself totally; gone on an indefinite leave as well.'

'Where does she work?'

'Cognizant; she is a programmer.'

'And you?'

'I'm a management professor at a private university in Salt Lake. What about you?'

'I work in a bank. So does my husband. Different banks though.'

'How is your husband taking it?'

The response was pretty late.

'He is pretending that whatever has happened can be forgotten, that we should move on. That's how he is taking it,' she said, frowning. She felt as if Shayan had smirked and turned to look at him.

'You know my wife and I had a love marriage. We thought we were soulmates. We thought we were always on the same page. And we sure were. But it took us a few years of married life to realize we were on the same page of two very different books.'

Priyanjali felt overwhelmed. Hers had been an arranged marriage and she had never felt that her husband and she were ever on the same page. Till now her marriage had been a constant struggle to be on the same page. But which page was that? Where was it? When would she find it? She had no answers. When Binny had been born she had thought that they were close to that page but now that her son was gone she felt that she would never find that elusive page.

Priyanjali's phone rang. She picked it up and answered something in a low voice. Shayan couldn't hear anything.

'Husband's home. I'll have to leave now. Bye,' Priyanjali said and, without waiting for a response, left.

They didn't say it but they both knew that they would there in the park the next day at the same time. What Priyanjali didn't know, and Shayan did, was that he had lied to her about their children's friendship.

* * *

Chapter Three

When Priyanjali came to the park the next evening, she saw Shayan sitting with a box on his lap. He waved at her. Instead of waving, she gave him a tight-lipped smile. By the time she reached the bench, she knew what was on his lap.

'It's Titu's birthday. His mother is unreachable. I couldn't help but cut a cake. Then I thought I may not be alone in this park.' He looked at Priyanjali. She didn't meet his eyes and instead sat beside him.

'What's the flavour?'

'Black Forest, his favourite.'

'Let's open it.'

Shayan opened the box, planted a small candle in the cake and lighted it.

'May I request you to blow it?'

'Me?'

'Titu loved your Maggi noodles.'

Priyanjali smiled and blew out the candle. Shayan cut a piece and held it up for Priyanjali to take a bite. But she instead politely took it from his hands.

'I guessed it would be Black Forest,' she said.

'How come?' Shayan's surprise was genuine.

'I realized last night that Binny used to write a diary. I found it while going through his stuff. I don't know how I didn't find it earlier.'

'Did he mention Titu?'

'Only on every other page. Black Forest was also there. I don't know why they didn't talk to each other during their karate class?'

'They did. You would drop and later pick up Binny, but I would sit through the class.'

'You did?'

Shayan nodded. 'I would find them doing all sorts of mischief. And then turning into gentlemen the moment the class got over.'

'Don't mind, but I'll take another piece. I don't know why but I really like sweets these days.'

'Sweets take care of the sorrow within,' Shayan said, and cut a piece for himself.

'Within here only,' Priyanjali said, pointing to her temples, and added, 'but never here.' She tapped on her chest a couple of times.

'Why didn't you have a second child?' Shayan asked. He knew it was too personal a question to ask, but he didn't apologize. He knew she would answer. Sooner or later.

'I had had complications during my first delivery. The doctor was pretty clear that I shouldn't conceive again. I was confident there won't be a need to. I was happy with Binny. He was my world.'

Blanketed in a warm darkness, the park bench exuded a certain emotional comfort. The warmth also made them abandon all formality.

'My wife and I didn't even try again. In fact, it has been long since we were intimate. I don't know how it happened, when it happened. It's as if it was all a dream and when we woke up we understood it was actually a nightmare. I don't think we will connect again, ever.'

'Do you want to connect with her again?'

'I don't know. Maybe, maybe not.'

'Do you think our children's death have exposed something about ourselves to us? Something that had better stayed hidden?'

'I think whatever was hidden was hidden for far too long. If it has surfaced, there must be a reason behind it, and we should respect it.'

'I agree,' Priyanjali sounded pensive.

'What if years later we realize what we thought was the reason wasn't really the real reason?'

'I have wondered about that. But I haven't been able to find a solution.'

'Maybe because solutions come to mind when we are actually in a problematic situation?'

'Maybe we find out solutions when we are seeking them with all our heart. Maybe right now we aren't seeking the situation with all our heart.'

Priyanjali's phone rang. When she was done, Shayan knew it was time for her to leave.

'Would you like to keep this? To combat the sorrow?' Shayan said with a smile, gesturing to his temples while offering her the remaining cake.

'I will let you try that for once,' Priyanjali said.

'Can't wait to tell you if it works.' It was an indirect way of telling each other that they will meet again.

Today Priyanjali had lied. Her son had had no diary. She had lied because she wanted to express, to connect to someone. There was an innate desire to get rid of the person she had become after the death of her son. While walking home, she wondered, in the process of getting rid of that person will she become a new one?

* * *

Chapter Four

Priyanjali arrived at the park at the same time the next evening. But the bench where Shayan and she usually sat was empty. She had become habituated to finding him sitting there. She walked around the park twice and then decided to leave. It was when she had just come out of the park that she found Shayan standing across the road. He briskly walked towards her.

'I'm sorry. I went for some work to south Kolkata. Took a cab but it broke down half a kilometre from here.'

The unasked-for justification told Priyanjali that he too thought their rendezvous was more than mere meetings.

'You came running?' she asked.

'I didn't want to miss you . . . in the park. That's all.'

'You sure you want to be in the park?'

'I wouldn't have come running otherwise.'

'Let's go back then. You need to sit down and catch your breath.'

They walked beside each other quietly till they reached the bench. This time Priyanjali sat closer to Shayan. Whether it was intentional or not, Shayan didn't know. He knew interpretations like these moulded one's mind, one's attitude towards another. Not that he wasn't interested in that moulding.

'The cake did help,' he said.

'I was sure it would.'

'Thanks, Priyanjali.' It was the first time he had taken her name.

'Don't mention it, Shayan,' she said.

'I feel like the days are simply flying away while I'm static. As if life has become a time-lapse video or whatever it's called. You know the kind which is shown in movies?'

'Yes, that's right. Are you into movies?'

'Not much. If I come across any interesting trailers, I make plans with my office team.'

'Not husband?'

'Oh, no! He invariably falls asleep in the theatre. It's better that he sleeps at home.'

The heaviness that had earlier characterized their conversations was slowly lifting. It was becoming progressively lighter. And they had the feeling of going with the flow. Such justifications were important for both of them because they didn't belong to each other the way they belonged to their spouses.

'What about you?' Priyanjali asked.

'I watch only Bengali art house films or world cinema. Not much into masala flicks.'

'You don't look that type either. I enjoy all kinds of movies though. Depends on what draws me in. I don't think I am that selective about my movies. I've seldom had niche tastes about anything. The same with food. I like everything.'

'And what about men? You like everyone?'

Priyanjali realized that Shayan was kidding.

'I'll be so judged if I said yes right now.'

'Not really judged. But generalizations in certain aspects kill all rays of hope.'

'Now I know why you had a love marriage.'

'Really? Why?'

'You are good with words. I'm sure you could woo women easily.'

'Didn't try to woo many. The one I tried to became my wife.'

'Are you sad that you didn't?'

'I'm not sad but I'm a man. The itch will always be there. Whether I act upon it or not is different.'

'I like that you are so honest about it.'

'Does that tick something off your list?'

'God, are we flirting?'

They burst out laughing but Priyanjali stopped abruptly.

'You know I'm laughing after nearly a month and a half?'

'That's true for me as well.' But unlike Priyanjali, Shayan didn't sound so uptight. Their conversation was cut short by a third person, an elderly gentleman, who sat beside Priyanjali. Realizing that she was feeling awkward, Shayan stood up.

'Let's take a walk.'

They walked around the park. No words were exchanged. When two people are comfortable with each other's silences, there is often a latent, unfiltered chemistry waiting to surface. Shayan noticed her glance at her phone a few times. He understood that perhaps she was checking the time.

'No call from your husband today?' he asked.

'He isn't in the city for the next few days,' she said and added after a few seconds as she turned towards the exit, 'but my mother is. I told her I was going out to buy vegetables. My brother and his wife are visiting us for dinner. They think I can't handle it alone.'

'It's strange but we are always stronger than our near and dear ones think we are.'

'That's because they love us.'

'And love makes us weak.'

'Depends,' she said with a smile, and took her leave. When she crossed the road, she heard Shayan yell, 'Tomorrow I'll be on time.'

She smile and disappeared into another lane.

* * *

Chapter Five

'Have you ever been jealous of someone's luck?' Priyanjali asked. They were sitting on the bench.

'I have been jealous of people more than their luck,' Shayan said.

'Last night during dinner I kept looking at my brother's wife. I'm jealous of her luck.'

'Why? What does she have that you don't?'

'Happiness. Unadulterated happiness. She looks so damn, genuinely happy.'

'Is it because of . . . ?'

'Not just because of Binny's death. It has always been this way. It is because of these negative feelings that I think I deserve the situation I'm in right now.'

'You're forgetting, Priyanjali, that you're not alone. It's you, me and all those other parents who lost their children that day.'

There were a few minutes of silence.

'You're right,' she said. 'I thought so to validate my negativity. We always seek reasons to cover up our dark side, isn't it? Maybe I'm an inherently jealous person. If you don't mind, may I ask you something?' Priyanjali looked at him.

'Sure.'

'Were you ever involved romantically with anyone other than your wife?'

'No. It has been ten years since we saw each other, met, dated, married and had a son. I've never been involved with anyone else. What about you?'

'I did date a boy back in college, but you know how it was back then. Nobody is that serious even if they pretend to be. I always knew it wouldn't fructify.'

'I understand. And by fructify you mean marriage?'

'Yes, marriage. My husband and I have been married for a little over a decade now.'

'Did you have any affairs or flings in between?'

'No, nothing. Tell me something . . . '

The way Priyanjali was steering the conversation made Shayan realize how clogged her mind was. Not that his was sorted, but he decided to hold on to his questions for the time being and listen to her patiently. Patience had always been his virtue.

'What do you do when after investing so much time and emotion into a relationship, you realize it's not working out?' The eagerness with which she asked the question made Shayan realize that she had needed an answer for a long time.

'What else can you do except for getting on with life?'

'Easier said than done.'

'I know, but . . .'

'Won't the fear of probably reaching a dead end curtail one's instinct of giving the feelings you feel for someone a try?'

'We always take away newer fears from an old broken relationship. And more often than not inject it into the next one. And sometimes we lose the opportunity for a new relationship because we are a little too scared.'

'I think that happens because what all of us want is a destination. Or at least the promise of one, isn't it?'

'Agreed. That promise is so important to all of us. We just can't take a ride without knowing where we're heading. If not exactly, at least a vague idea. That helps us decide how much time and emotion we should invest.'

'And yet deep inside we know that that promise is nothing but an illusion. Who has seen the future? Who knows it? The truth is anything can go wrong at any time.

That's how vulnerable we are. How can we be sure of something when the system we live in is so chaotic?'

'We can only look back at things when they have happened and tell ourselves that they had to happen. That's all that we can do. Right now I look back at my marriage and realize that it had to fall apart. When it was in the process of falling apart, I had no clue. In retrospection, I can see the clues without any difficulty.'

'I have always wondered why isn't being in a relationship an end in itself? A relationship that has no future but only the present.' Priyanjali glanced at Shayan; he looked amused.

'I'm talking shit, isn't it?'

'No, no. You are saying stuff a man will love to hear. We hate a future where we are tethered to just one woman.'

'Such dogs!' Priyanjali blurted out.

'I'm sorry. I was kidding.'

'I'm sorry. I shouldn't have said that. I don't usually utter profanities.'

'Then I'm glad I could squeeze something rare out of you.'

'Do you realize how smooth you are at flirting?'

'Do you think it happens as smoothly with everyone?'

'There you go again. Huh!'

Shayan laughed. At that moment his phone rang. He took it out of his trousers' pocket and as soon as he saw the name of the caller, he stopped laughing.

'Excuse me.' He stood up and walked ahead to take the call. Priyanjali kept looking at him. He seemed a little withdrawn. Shayan finished the call within a minute. In that minute he listened more than he talked. Then he came back.

'You have to excuse me today. My wife is back. I'll have to go.'

Priyanjali felt like a child whose soap bubbles had burst at the same time.

* * *

Chapter Six

She was in two minds about visiting the park that evening. What if Shayan hadn't come? She didn't want to be disappointed. At work, she decided not to go to the park. But when the time came, as if she was under a spell, she took a cab straight to the park from office. But she didn't get out of it till she spotted Shayan sitting on the bench.

'I thought you will not come today.'

'My wife didn't come to stay with me. She was there to collect a few things that she had forgotten earlier.'

'So she left again?' Priyanjali asked as she sat beside him.

Shayan nodded. 'This morning,' he said.

'Why is she behaving like that?'

'I don't know. I don't want to know.'

'Doesn't she realize leaving you right now will harm your relationship even more?'

'Maybe she wants it that way? Maybe she wants me to end it because no matter how much she wants it herself, she will never the guts to say it? It can be anything. We are so complex. We say something, mean something else and desire something completely different.'

'Hmm, I agree. Even I'm not that open with my husband. At least your wife is still expressing herself through her actions. I'm not even capable of doing that. I will never be able to leave him and stay with my parents.'

'What's stopping you?'

'I am. Even if I want to I can't just live for myself or take selfish decisions. Other lives are attached to mine. And my one action is bound to affect the people connected to me. If I go to my parents' house and tell them my husband and I have always been incompatible, they will not understand. Nor will the society that they are answerable to. Incompatibility isn't a good enough reason to leave one's husband. And invariably I'll be written off as someone who couldn't handle her marriage.'

'So you fear the society?'

'Don't you?'

'I'm not sure about fear but it does amputate the real me at different levels. The real me knows it's over with my wife but the one that abides by the rules of the society may carry on living like this for I don't know how many years. Maybe for the rest of my life.'

'You had a love marriage; perhaps you will be able to answer this. We human beings need companionship; we are hopeless without co-habitation, but tell me does familiarity breed contempt? Do we stop being attractive to our partners over time?'

Shayan thought for some time. She didn't pester him for an answer. They were looking at other people in the park.

'I think an emotional blindness does set in,' Shayan finally said.

'Emotional blindness,' Priyanjali repeated and added, 'I like this term. It explains a lot without any elaborate explanation.'

'The moment we know someone is there, who won't leave us voluntarily, the blindness starts setting in. We only have the person we know in front of us and not the one the person can be.'

'I didn't get the last part.'

'When I met my wife last night she was certain that all I do these days is go to college to teach and come back home. Nothing in between. She can never imagine me meeting a friend and talking to her like this in a park.'

'That's because you will be the person she knows you to be and not the one you can be?'

'Precisely.'

'I would have loved to have this discussion with my husband. But I know he won't be interested.'

'Or maybe you *think* he won't be interested. Maybe you need to know a different him?'

Priyanjali suddenly felt a pang of guilt. *What if Shayan was right?*

'I think I should leave now.'

'Your husband is back?'

'No. But I have some official work to finish.'

Shayan wanted to request her to stay for five more minutes but she seemed edgy; she wouldn't have considered his request.

* * *

Chapter Seven

'I tried last night but I was right about my husband. He doesn't like getting into the thick of things too much,' Priyanjali said. They were taking a stroll around the park as the bench was occupied by a couple. But they had their eyes on it.

'That's why he will always be happier than you.'

'You're right. People who avoid getting too involved with everything are always happier as compared to others. That's why he handled himself so much better than me after Binny's death. I'm not saying it didn't damage him.

I'm sure it did but unlike me he didn't seek a reason behind the damage. I did. He accepted things the way they were; I still haven't been able to.'

'Or maybe he isn't that expressive? Maybe he pretends to be okay so you may not suffer more?'

'I like the way you take his side most of the time. You need not but you still do. Really commendable.' They exchanged a smile. Walking side by side seemed better than sitting beside each other. But the bench was empty now. However, Priyanjali didn't propose the idea of sitting on it. Nor did Shayan.

'To be honest I'm supporting myself here,' he said.

'As in?'

'Since Titu's death I've actually revisited my relationship with my wife a lot of times, trying to understand that which I think has changed and can be mended. It has made me wonder about a lot of possibilities. But alas! It's so difficult to predict how someone is.'

'And you have had a love marriage. Imagine my condition. Mine was arranged.'

Shayan chuckled gently.

'I don't think we are heading towards a split,' Priyanjali said.

'Were you contemplating it?'

'Honestly, I was. I think it was because of Binny that we didn't break up. Now that he isn't there any more and the fact that I can't conceive again did make me feel that we should separate. Without Binny, we have no common thread.'

'I think that's where we falter. We always make it mandatory for our spouse to have the same tastes as us.'

'You don't think so?'

'I think a relationship works out best when a couple is tolerant of each other's differences; it is more important than having shared interests. Yet we keep looking for them and when we can't find them, we tell ourselves we aren't made for each other.'

'Do you really believe in the whole made-for-each-other thing?'

'As I said it is all about affinity, a natural chemistry, rapport. Why do you think we have been meeting for days now?' Priyanjali stopped. Shayan paused after taking a few steps ahead of her.

'We have a good rapport?' she asked.

'Don't you think so?' he said, walking back towards her.

'I think so. But what do we do about it?'

'Do we have to do something about it? Why can't we just let it be?'

'Like the kind of relationship that only stays alive in the present and fades into oblivion the moment we bid each other goodbye?'

'Somewhat like that.'

Priyanjali was walking towards the park's exit. Shayan followed her.

'I'll be gone for the weekend to my mother's place. I will be back on Monday.'

'I'll wait for you on the bench,' Shayan said. Their eyes locked on each other.

'Not here. Not where we visited with our children. We are friends now, right?'

Shayan seemed lost for a moment. Then regaining his composure, said, 'Two married people, kind of disconnected with their spouses, with dead children . . . I don't think the society will see it as a friendship.'

'To hell with society then. Give me your number. I will text you where we can meet on Monday.'

Priyanjali and Shayan happily exchanged numbers.

'With very few people do we strike the right chord in a relationship,' Priyanjali said. 'A little here and we become partners. A little there and we turn into strangers. Right now we are both strangers and partners. That's an interesting point to be in, right?'

'I'll wait for the text, Priyanjali,' Shayan said.

Priyanjali smiled and left the park.

On Bed with Strangers

Sneha
Date: 6 October
Time: Night
Place: Bedroom

It's funny when you don't know a person at all. I mean *at all*. And still want to have sex with him.

The lights are out. Tonight, I'm on bed with . . . I won't you tell you his name. Let him be for you what he is for me: a stranger. I use carpool while going to office. I met him on one such trip. And right now I'm having sex with him. He is what I thought he would be in bed: a savage. I like it; I have always liked it this way. But my husband never understood it; he couldn't live up to my expectations as he wasn't interested. But I always knew what my body was capable of. I always wanted sex to be the language through which I understood my body and soul. But all that I could manage was some acquired knowledge. Where is the experience? Where is the feeling? I had read somewhere that sex is less about the organs involved in it than it is about the mind. I agree. But the problem is in finding someone who too believes in this. No man likes to match a woman on that level. And even if he does, he invariably ends up judging her sooner or later. That's why there's no experience. No feeling. That's why I chose this man tonight.

I moan loudly as he makes me come by eating me. At first I feel scared that the neighbours might hear me. Then a smile appears on my face. At least someone made me feel as wild as I felt I was.

* * *

Shekhar
Date: 6 October
Time: Night
Place: Bedroom

The one brutal truth that I can't tell my wife, Sneha, is that I have no motivation to get intimate with her any more. I don't get an erection even when I see her naked.

The lights are out. Tonight, I'm with a friend of Sneha's in our bedroom. You don't know her so why bother with her name? I knew this woman since Sneha and I started dating, but it's only recently that I thought of sleeping with her. I don't know what exactly drew me to her. Maybe I needed another option and she was the easiest. And she hasn't been disappointing at all. The way her tongue slithers down my chest to my groin makes me wonder why the same act when performed by Sneha fails to elicit any response from my body. Are we so used to each other that the sacred, unsaid unpredictability that keeps the spark alive in a marriage is dead?

Sex is such a primal urge. And we can feel the need to satiate the urge with so many people. When we do, we feel guilty about it. If we tell others, we are made to feel immoral. I don't understand why humans weren't designed to distinguish between love and lust. Why do we have to see one through the lens of the other? *Always*! If I don't lust for Sneha any more, my love for her is compromised, or so the world will like me to believe. It doesn't matter how much I love her, if I don't get it up for her, the society will judge me. And then people say sex isn't important. Fuck them! My mind goes blank as Sneha's friend blows me, making me come.

* * *

Sneha
Date: 20 October
Time: Night
Place: Bedroom

I'm loving this: to be with a stranger in my bed. And witness how my body reacts to the thought of different people.

The lights are out. I'm with a man I saw the other night in a pub when I was there with my husband, Shekhar. I didn't know then that I would end up in the sack with him. Unlike the carpool commuter, this man is gentle, but he is good with foreplay. I like that. A man should respect a woman's mood when it comes to sex. If she is in the mood to tumble around, play rough, only then should it be that way. I rarely struck that balance with Shekhar. When I'd want it rough, he'd come too quickly. When I'd want it to be slow and sensual, he'd want to jump on me and devour me like a sex doll. With time I stopped expecting anything. I surrendered to his mood else the sex only got worse. But this man sure knows how to build things up. Like a novel. Chapter after chapter till we reach the climax. I hate men who try to climax in the first chapter itself. Make a woman feel like a detailed and engaging read, and watch what she does for you. But no. All that some men like Shekhar know is to finish things.

There's an intoxicating magic in prolonging the inevitable. Who will teach this to these men? Where's the experience? Where's the feeling?

I know he is reaching the climax. He is thrusting faster now. In no time our insides shatter, which can only be put together after a deep sleep.

* * *

Shekhar
Date: 20 October
Time: Night
Place: Bedroom

Will I be a freak if I say the girl I'm with tonight resembles Sneha when she was in her early twenties? And that's the only reason why I'm with her?

The lights are out. *Why* did I choose a girl who resembles a younger Sneha? Does that mean I miss her? Could be. The younger Sneha was an enigma; the one I've been living with for the last ten years is a thoroughly read book. There were reasons for me to go back to the enigma, there's no reason for me to consider the present Sneha, even though I have looked for reasons a lot of times. I want our marriage to work out but when I ask myself why . . . nothing comes to mind. Till our fifth year I used to say it's because of love that we are together, but now I know it is possible to feel entirely nothing for the person you share your domestic life with. We just don't say it aloud. Who will say it first? Who will ask for a divorce? Who will answer questions by our parents, friends, the society? Too much emotional labour. Better to go on pretending everything was exactly the way it was when we'd met for the first time. But we know in our hearts that the fairy tale got over a long time ago. At least I know that.

Honestly, Sneha was better than this girl at her age. This one is a novice. I have to tell her a lot of things. Who likes to explain so much while having sex? Is this a college lecture? Sneha was a natural in bed. And yet how things have changed. Or maybe I have.

* * *

Sneha
Date: 1 November
Time: Night
Place: Bedroom

Will I be considered wicked if I confess that I've been comparing the strangers I've been having sex with, with my husband and getting a kick out of it?

The lights are out. Tonight I'm with a college friend of mine. He told me he had been fantasizing about me for years now. I'm certain I'll get multiple orgasms tonight. A rarity for me. I remember the time when Shekhar used to devour me. His performance has decreased over the years. Am I not attractive any more? Then how come these men show such intense interest in me? Is attraction subjective? Maybe it is short-lived. Anyone who has been in love will know the difference between lusty fucking and love making. There was a time Shekhar and I did the former, then it became the latter and now it is neither. We do it because we feel we owe each other something as husband and wife. But we never give each other what we really require: honesty. Why can't we tell each other that 'we are done' as casually and easily as we had once professed our love for each other? To let go of a person you once loved with all your heart so that she can have a free life is also part of the responsibility stemming out of the love you once felt for her, right?

Tonight was bad. My college friend fell short of my expectations. But then, I wonder, both Shekhar and I have too fallen short of our own expectations of each other. Who can be blamed in such a case? I find that my eyes are moist. I don't know why. I didn't want to . . .

* * *

Shekhar
Date: 1 November
Time: Night
Place: Bedroom

How can you deliberately hurt someone? That too someone with whom you have had the most beautiful memories of your life? And that's why I cannot tell Sneha that we are done.

The lights are out. Tonight, I don't care who I'm with. All right, I had spurned this woman once, chosen Sneha over her. Back then I was in love with my wife. But this woman claims to still be in love with me. I can't claim the same for Sneha. Is it because we have already had what this woman couldn't and didn't? The fundamental difference between lust and love is that the former dies if sated and the latter only fades if requited. And what fades may well become prominent some day. That is why love is more dangerous, I believe. What if my love for Sneha resurfaces after I tell her we are done? How will I be able to get her back then? I can't take the claims of this woman seriously because we haven't lived together for ten years. Domestic life changes a lot of things. The first being how you look at your partner. She transforms from someone desirable to someone so bloody achievable and approachable that all sense of an adventure is killed. We are all vagabonds, hunting souls. Adventure is important in domesticity whether we realize it or not. Hunger is what made us hunt for food. The mind makes us hunt for the body. Marriage is a cleverly designed blinker for our wild desires. We know there's so much outside it but aren't allowed to look.

I only pretend I liked the session with her. I flash the same fake smile at her as the one I give to Sneha after coming back from office. Has she understood it? If so, why isn't she confronting me about it? I wonder as the post-coital bliss soon lulls me to sleep.

* * *

Sneha and Shekhar
Date: 15 November
Time: Night
Place: Their bedroom

Lights are on.

Sneha and Shekhar are with each other in bed. They don't talk much these days. Ten years of being together has eaten into their once romanticized idea of togetherness. Only humans are capable of churning out such ironies. They are lying side by side. Some small talk is made about how the day went, how work was, a little gossip, some news about their relatives, and then one of them yawns. The other understands it's time to say good night.

Sneha turns around, her back to Shekhar. She feels his hand on her shoulder. Their touch has a new language these days. She grasps his hand. The new language is a little confusing at times. Shekhar switches off the lights. In their minds they are with strangers. They surrender themselves to these unknown people in their bed.

For how long will they communicate with cryptic gestures hoping that the other will bring up the issue at hand? Shekhar wonders.

Where are the words? Sneha wonders.

Suddenly, Shekhar thinks about the woman who moved into the flat next door. Sneha thinks about the man she saw at a colleague's marriage last week. Both husband and wife switch off from each other's reality.

Acknowledgements

I had always wanted to come up with a short story collection, where I could write about myriad people in different situations bound by a common theme. 'No man is an island'; what touches me could also touch someone else somewhere. Perhaps it's our reaction to different stimuli that makes our stories different. *Cheaters* took a lot out of me because it was a task to strip down the characters to their bare minimum and reveal them in their emotional nudity. Even though this collection had been at the back of my mind for some time now, it wouldn't have possibly reached you, my readers, without the help and support of certain individuals.

The foremost being Milee. Thank you so much for showing faith in this collection as well as the storyteller in me time and again. Such an experiment is next to impossible to conduct in the commercial zone without the love and support of an enterprising publisher like you.

Thank you, Indrani, my editor, for bringing your value to the collection and also for letting me know that you found the flavour of the magnificent Buddhadeb Basu in the stories. You don't know how happy you made me feel that day. Cheers!

The entire sales team at Penguin Random House India: Nandan, Vijesh, Pinaki da, Nirmalya da, Gopal, Harish bhai, Sunil, Raghavendra, Saleheen. And my publicists: Sudhanshu and Peter. A heartfelt thanks to you guys for the constant support.

Gratitude to my family for always being there.

To my close friends who need not be named here: double thumbs-up for the love in all situations and seasons.

To all those boys/men and girls/women (sorry, I can't name them for that would be a breach of trust) who opened up to me and poured their hearts out, making their darkest confessions about their marriages and partners. Cues from these make up the stories in this collection.

Special mention: Thank you, *Ranisa*, for those soul-stirring conversations. Who else can emotionally disturb me as well as satiate me at the same time?

R—every moment with you is a realization. And the ones without you are a lesson. I can now safely say that we don't belong to each other. We *ARE* each other. Thank you!